Politics Makes Strange Deadfellows

Book Two in the Kate Matthews Mystery Series

By

Jane DiLucchio

ISBN 978-1-61929-466-0

Cover Design by AcornGraphics

Editors Verda Foster & Nann Dunne

Publisher's Note:

Acknowledgments

Thanks go to many people and entities for their help with this book.

Holly Perea, Executive Assistant to the Mayor and Council of Santa Barbara, who gave generously of her time and knowledge. Hopefully, she will forgive me for bending some of the information she gave me about how the council works. This is, after all, a work of fiction.

Joshua Morton, Lieutenant, Investigations, City of Santa Barbara, Police Department explained the missing persons process to me. Any police procedural errors are mine alone.

Jean Scott, Maureen McLaughlin, Maureen Serra, Doug Heumann, Eveline Blanchette, Laura DiLucchio, Kathy Kreyns, Laurie Gillis, and Sue Stimpson have my sincere gratitude for beta reading, editing, feedback, and friendship.

Verda Foster and Nann Dunne, many thanks for excellence in editing and for exhibiting unending patience with me.

Flashpoint Publications and Patty Schramm, thank you for your help and your encouragement and for giving Kate a home.

Loving thanks go to Serra's Sisters, for unconditionally supporting me throughout this whole adventure called life.

Dedication

To Sue Stimpson, my love, my life, and my greatest supporter. Thank you.

Chapter One

I thought about strangling Julia Thompson. And it wasn't the first time. As mayor of Santa Barbara, Thompson claimed the right to respond first to any proposal presented by the staff at the weekly City Council meeting. Today, she ripped apart a suggestion to redirect funds used by the police to deal with the homeless problem. Her diatribe clocked four and a half minutes already—nearing five, I corrected, as I glanced down at my watch again. The urge to choke her vied with one to yawn. Loudly.

"Kate, staring daggers at Julia won't stop her." Reynaldo Sanchez, the representative from district five, whispered into my ear. "She knows better than to acknowledge you."

I swiveled slightly in my, thankfully, padded woven chair and murmured, "Here I thought I was being so discreet."

"Not with the scowls and checking your watch every thirty seconds."

I faced forward, sighed, and tried to focus on Thompson's tirade. She must have noticed my previous inattention, for her next words were directed to me.

"Even Ms. Matthews, the representative from the second district," Thompson said, waving her hand in my direction, "has to understand the importance of ridding our city of unsafe, unsightly, and dehumanizing camps of those who choose to squat in the streets and parks of our city."

I didn't rise to the bait but merely looked out across the sparse crowd in the City Council chambers. Our regular Tuesday afternoon meetings weren't exactly the hottest tickets in town. But each held at least one chunk of important business in it. Unfortunately, Mayor Thompson liked to make every meeting about her rather than the city. It was an ongoing argument between us ever since I was elected to the council three months ago.

Before the mayor could continue, the door at the back of

the chambers flew open. A young, white male in jeans and a faded, blue shirt careened into the room, a shoulder bag hanging down his right side. He stared straight up at the platform on which we sat. His sun-bleached, brown, wavy hair was neatly combed straight back from his pale, taut, angular face. His dark eyes glared up at those of us seated on the stage.

Thompson's eyes grew wide, and she beckoned to the police officer who stood to the side behind the council members. The officer hustled toward the entryway, but before she reached the intruder, the man pulled an oversized gun out of the shoulder bag and shouted, "You all deserve to die!"

"Down!" I yelled.

Even as my fellow council members dove for cover, a blast erupted from the gun. Red spread across Thompson's chest.

****

"An animal rights activist," I said to Alicia after I returned home from the aborted meeting. I shook my head. "You'd think they'd realize humans are animals, too. It's not such a great idea to go around shooting them." I petted the orange tabby that was stretched across my lap as I sat on the living room couch. Ginger looked up at me as if weighing my words on the relative worth of humans. We must have passed muster, for she closed both eyes again and began to purr. "At least it was only a paint ball. Julia will need to buy a new shirt, but she didn't have any physical damage other than a sore chest. Who knew those things packed such a wallop?"

Alicia reached across the couch and squeezed my hand. "I'm proud of you for ducking instead of charging the shooter." She brushed my graying, brown hair back from the edge of my face. "That was a rare moment of maturity on your part."

I doubted the full videotape of the meeting would ever be aired. If it did, I hated to think what my wife's reaction would be to the scene of me hauling the paint-spattered mayor behind the oak dais before racing off the stage to tackle the shooter. Luckily, several citizens and the police officer subdued the ranting young man before I arrived at the back of the council chamber.

I tried for an innocent look. "That's me. Mature to the max. Besides, I've got too much to live for. You, our kids, and the world's cutest granddaughter. What more can one ask of life?"

Alicia lifted one eyebrow. "You little shit. You did go after him, didn't you?"

Red crept up my neck, but I gave her my most solemn look. "I swear I had nothing to do with taking him down."

Sometimes Alicia is able to follow my carefully worded omissions. It's the by-product of us being together for over twenty years. I could tell she was applying her mental GPS tracking ability now. Her chestnut-brown eyes narrowed, and she studied my face. "That doesn't mean you didn't try." She released my hand and whacked my arm. "Someday, Katherine May Matthews, you're going to grow up. Hopefully, before you get yourself killed."

Her cell phone rang and stopped Alicia from hurling more abuse my way. She merely gave me an exasperated glare before sliding her phone from her front pocket.

I heard our son Ben's muted voice over the line.

"Yes, she's fine. Let me put you on speaker." Alicia punched the appropriate button, and Ben's baritone rang clear in the room.

"I was watching the news. Ma, you looked so rad tackling the mayor."

"Rad was the very look I was going for." I gave Alicia a sheepish shrug. "Where did you see this?"

"The local news has the council chamber's feed playing over and over. And there's cell phone footage of the shooter being flattened. Don't know how you got down there so fast. You looked ready to jump on the pile holding him down."

A beeping interrupted Ben. Not soon enough from my point of view. Sarah, our daughter, was on the other line.

We repeated my lack of injuries to Sarah, and she repeated the news of the television coverage. Her take on the events was a little different. "What were you thinking, Ma? That guy could have had a real gun with real bullets. You could've been killed. What would we have told little Amy then?"

"You could tell Amy the tale of how one of her grandmothers heroically saved Santa Barbara from a lunatic, animal rights advocate."

Sarah's snort was audible over the phone. "I'll let Mom deal with you on that comment. They've identified the shooter. His name is Jeffrey Henderson, and he's a member of Animals First. They're kind of like PETA on steroids."

"That's all we need," I grumbled. "Wackos weighing in on the Shoreline Park issue."

Sarah disagreed, as I expected she would. "Even wacko fringe groups have times they're right. Poisoning those ground squirrels will disrupt the food chain and probably lead to large carnivores dying off."

Sarah was a budding environmental lawyer. And sometimes a severe trial to an ex-corporate lawyer like me. "Even if I agreed with that scenario, I'm not sure assassinating the mayor is a good way to make that point."

"Probably not, but something's got to be done to stop the poisoning."

One unique aspect of governing a seaside community is the attempted preservation of cliff-sides that seem determined to fall into the ocean no matter what one does. Most of the time, rain caused the problems, but sometimes Mother Nature sent other little helpers along. Ground squirrels have tunneled through Santa Barbara's Shoreline Park for years, but the land was now unstable from their actions and erosion of the seaside cliff accelerated yearly. The poisoning plan was put into operation a month before I got onto the City Council.

"I'm working with Reynaldo Sanchez, the city manager, and the Humane Society on a different course of action for dealing with the ground squirrels. But we'll still need the agreement of at least five members to pass the motion. Protestors doing idiotic stunts is not going to help the cause."

"That's a shame because little Amy is going to be so photogenic at the next eco-rally. I'm thinking of dressing her like a squirrel."

Chapter Two

Santa Barbara, California, is home to many things: festivals, theaters, museums, hiking trails, and ocean-going activities. It also claims to have more parks per resident than any other city in the United States. I don't know if that's true, but I do know there are a lot of them and they're well-used.

Sunday mornings were my time to watch our granddaughter, Amy, while her mom studied for her last year of classes at law school and Alicia, a realtor, held open houses in the nearby town of Goleta. First thing after breakfast, I loaded Amy into her high-tech baby stroller and we wandered through one of those many parks.

Despite Oak Park's name, it was mainly filled with sycamore trees that shaded the dirt paths that wound through the rolling landscape. Since it was one of those rare weekends when no cultural fair was held, Amy and I had the green and leafy space mainly to ourselves.

I decided to go off the cement pathway for our adventure. Amy's stroller was designed for all-terrain travel, and she seemed to enjoy bumping over the ruts of the narrow dirt path.

"Watch the birdies fly by. Can you hear them? Each one has a different sound." I kept up my end of the one-sided conversation. Amy, at four months of age, didn't contribute a lot besides the occasional burble.

"And what do you think that is? See the red flowers? Someday your grandma is going to learn what all these plants and birds are, so that when your language skills improve, you're going to be so impressed with my knowledge of nature."

Amy chose that moment to kick and chortle. I took that as approval for my educational plans.

"And what do you think this blue in the bush is? It doesn't look like a flower, does it? Let's see." I wheeled her carriage closer to the edge of the trail then quickly drew it back, whipping it around so that Amy faced in the opposite direction. I knelt down, reached under the bush, and felt the neck of the still body. The skin was cold, and no pulse beat under it. I fumbled for my cell phone and dialed 911. "There's a man here at Oak Park. He's face down in the bushes beside one of the main trails. I think he's dead."

****

"It was Jeffrey Henderson, the protestor from Tuesday night," I said.

Our family was gathered in our living room. Sarah, who'd driven over as soon as she got the news, sat clutching Amy. They were on one of the tan, upholstered side chairs that usually faced the picture windows with a view of the ocean beyond. Sarah turned it to face the couch where her mother and I sat. Ben, who broke away from a pick-up basketball game at the news, perched on the edge of the love seat, hunched over as if ready to leap into action.

I'd called Alicia right after calling the police. I figured— correctly as it turned out—that Amy and I would be delayed in returning home. The police allowed Alicia to pick up Amy and take her home while I stayed for questioning. In the midst of their interrogation of me, the coroner arrived. They pushed back the bushes around his head, which previously obscured my vision of his profile. I recognized the young man's face immediately.

"The detectives recognized him as well. They said he made bail on Thursday." I gave Alicia's hand a squeeze before standing and striding over to the windows. The sight of the grey-blue undulations of the ocean usually calmed me. Today, it didn't do the trick. "Somebody did not like that guy. They really wanted him dead." The image of the dried blood that encircled the dime-sized exit wound in the boy's back made me slightly queasy.

Ben asked, "Any way it could have been an accident?"

"I don't think it was an accident and probably not suicide, either, since the police didn't find a weapon. At least, not while I was there."

Alicia sighed. "Thankfully, this time the police can't possibly think you had anything to do with it."

Her prediction was almost correct.

An hour later, while Sarah tried to get Amy to go down for a nap in the guest room, the doorbell rang. I hastened to answer the door, more to prevent the noise from disturbing Amy than to find out who wanted entrance. Two men in brown suits stood on our front porch. One of them was an old nemesis of mine, Police Detective Sam Levine.

"Hello, Ms. Matthews. I don't know if you remember me." Levine flipped open his ID case, and a picture of his lined face and close-cropped, grey hair stared back at me.

"It's kind of hard to forget someone who tried to charge me with murder, Detective."

Levine didn't rise to the bait, nor did he seem eager to waltz down memory lane to last year's murder of one of my massage clients. Instead, he indicated the Hispanic man to his left. "This is Detective Ruiz. We're looking for your stepdaughter, Sarah Wise Silver."

"Come in." I spoke the words automatically, my brain still processing the term he used. Stepdaughter. I'd never thought of Sarah in that way. It was a disquieting thought. Probably no more disquieting than having the police on our doorstep asking to speak to that self-same stepdaughter, but I wasn't quite focused on that. That is, until I asked the two men to sit down and the suspicious hemisphere of my brain fired up. "What do you need Sarah for?"

"We have a few questions for her. She wasn't at work, at school, or at home, so her husband suggested we try here." Levine cocked his head. "Is she here?"

"She's putting her daughter down for a nap." I settled myself on a side chair, making it clear I was in no hurry to go fetch her. "What's the problem?"

"We just want to ask her a few—"

"Questions. I know. In regard to what?" I said, careful to keep my voice and face bland. It wasn't unlike questioning a hostile witness. Be calm. In control. Relentless.

The detective employed the same skills. Levine merely asked, "Would you mind asking her to join us here?"

At that moment, Sarah appeared in the doorway, which

saved me from refusing a direct request. I gathered she recognized the police for being who they were. She swung to face me. "Now what did you do?"

Her voice sounded half bantering and half worried.

Before I could reply, Detective Levine said, "Ms. Silver? We're actually here to speak with you."

"Me?" Sarah folded into a chair next to me. "Is David okay?"

"It's not about your husband. It's about a man by the name of Jeffrey Henderson." He paused. When Sarah didn't respond, he asked, "Have you ever heard of him?"

"Of course I have. He's the one who shot the mayor." She waved at me. "The one my mom found dead in the park this morning."

Levine glanced over at me before settling his eyes on Sarah again. "Have you any dealings with Mr. Henderson?"

"Dealings? I'd never even heard of him until Tuesday night's council meeting nonsense."

"Any reason why he'd have your business card in his pocket?"

"My card?" Sarah looked flabbergasted. "You mean the one for Earth Ethics?" she asked, naming the environmental law firm she was clerking at.

The detective nodded. "He seems to have an appointment with you."

Sarah shook her head. "Not to my knowledge."

Levine wrote something in his notebook. "Are you active in any animal rights groups?"

"I support several monetarily, but I don't have time to be active in any."

"Is Animals First one of those?"

"No." Sarah looked as if she were about to add something then clamped her mouth shut.

Detective Ruiz finally joined the party. "Ma'am, we'd really appreciate anything you could tell us about Jeffrey Henderson. Maybe you met him at a party or something."

Sarah's headshake was firm. "I saw him on the news when he shot up the City Council meeting. That's the first and only time I've ever seen the man. He didn't look familiar at all. I've had no meetings with him whatsoever."

Detective Levine snapped his notebook shut and stood. "Then you'll have no objections to us checking your phone records, will you?"

I rose along with the detective. "Of course, she won't," I said, with a pleasant smile. "When you have a properly executed warrant."

****

The four of us gathered for a late lunch. We placed Amy's wooden crib by the dining room table where she played with her favorite stuffed bunny. Her nearness brought me a sense of comfort.

With the dishes cleared from the table, Ben broke the unspoken moratorium on discussing the murder. "Why didn't you let the police check Sarah's phone records? There's nothing to hide." He shot his sister a look. "You aren't having an affair or something, are you?"

Sarah jabbed his arm with her elbow.

I interrupted the sibling jousting match before it could escalate. "It's not about your sister's phone calls. It's about legal rights. We're losing our privacy rights in this country, and I refuse to add to that." I looked around the table at my family, and my heart beat faster. I was sure it was from feeling protective of them, but at the same time, I automatically checked for any other signs of another heart attack or an atrial fibrillation recurrence. No chest, jaw, neck, or arm pain. A return to normal rhythm eased my mind.

Alicia must have noticed my pause, for she reached over and stroked my arm. "You okay?"

I gave her my best reassuring smile. "I'm good." I leaned back in my chair and refolded my napkin into a neat rectangle. I felt my brain ease into an organized pattern of thought as I folded. I looked at Sarah. "Where might someone get your business card?"

Sarah brushed her hand through her sandy hair. As usual, her hair fell back into place as if a comb were expertly applied. "I've got several in my purse that I hand out. The office keeps a stack on the front counter, and I put some in a holder on my desk."

"So, this Henderson fellow could have come into the Earth Ethics office and picked one up." I frowned. "But why would the police think he made an appointment with you?"

"There's a place on the back of the card to fill out time and dates for appointments. Someone might have written something there, but why would they?"

"And there's no way to check your appointment calendar until you get back to the office tomorrow."

Both our children shot me incredulous looks.

Sarah stood and retrieved her purse. She dug for her phone and clicked it on. "My appointments are electronically entered into my calendar at work. That automatically syncs up with my online calendar." She pushed a few buttons and turned the phone around to face me.

A calendar with class schedules and various appointments filled the screen. I took the phone and scrolled through the dates. Jeffrey Henderson's name didn't appear on any of the dates within the next few weeks. I scrolled to today's date and handed the phone back to Sarah. "Are there any names you don't recognize on there?"

Sarah flicked her finger across the screen. "A few. But new clients are always coming in. Why?"

"If there really is a time and date on the card and we knew what they were, we could compare it to your client list."

Alicia looked at me, comprehension flooding her face. "You're thinking that someone else made the appointment for Henderson."

I shrugged. "It would be interesting to know who Henderson was working with."

Ben said, "Yep. Let's give the police someone else to scrutinize. The only one we don't want him connected to is Sarah."

Chapter Three

After my heart attack, I retired from my law practice and moved my family from Los Angeles to a beachfront home in Santa Barbara that I inherited from my parents. I returned to school and became a massage therapist, figuring it would be a relaxing way to make some extra cash. It hasn't always worked out that way, but I do enjoy it. But it became necessary to cut back my massage business when I was elected to the City Council. Actually, some of my clients dropped me. Something about not wanting me to see them naked now that I was in the public arena. I guess they didn't think of me as a real person who existed outside of the massage room until I started campaigning. Now that I gained some gravitas, it made them uncomfortable.

All that was fine with me. My true-blue clients stuck with me through the ugliness of last year, and they more than filled my shortened appointment calendar.

Red Boyle was one of those. That's why, despite the events of the morning, I felt determined to keep my massage appointment with her.

Now that I no longer got lost getting to her house, I enjoyed the late afternoon drive through the twisty, arboreal, back country lanes that dominated the exclusive enclave of Montecito, just south of Santa Barbara. The upcoming massage gave me something to think about other than Jeffrey Henderson's death and why he was in possession of Sarah's card.

Red's estate was one of the more modest ones. Only an acre of rolling hillside and a four-bedroom, mission-style adobe with a well-stocked wine cellar. Unlike most of her neighbors' homes, Red's included no pool, no ballroom, no movie theater. Wine, cats, and a much-younger boyfriend were not Red's only interests, but she spent a lot of time with all three.

True to her nickname, Red was a natural redhead, although grey was waging a war for dominance. She wore her usual yoga pants and a T-shirt, faded from years of washing. No makeup, no cosmetic surgery. Her wrinkled, freckled face beamed as I hefted my portable massage table from the trunk of my car. "All set up in the living room. C'mon in."

As I unfolded the table and put on the mattress cover and cotton sheets, Red left the room. She returned wrapped in a green kimono. I used the powder room to wash my hands as she slid onto the table face down and covered herself with the top sheet. After adjusting the neck cradle and arranging a bolster under her ankles, I warmed the eucalyptus-scented oil that was her favorite.

Effleurage is one of my favorite parts of massage. Spreading the oil in long, firm strokes along a person's back starts the connection of my hands to their skin and muscles. The sensory feedback of tenseness, relaxation, knots, and fluidity all combine to start the dance flow of pressure, kneading, and soothing that occurs when my hands are in sync with my client's body. Once I'm engaged in the process of massage, my mind enters a Zen zone of peace. My brain isn't busy thinking or analyzing. It observes but is detached. It floats, allowing my instincts to take over.

When I finished Red's massage with an energy-balancing ritual, I felt refreshed, like I had taken a sixty-minute nap. It struck me that my worrying over Sarah's tenuous connection to Henderson's murder definitely weighed me down. I was grateful to Red for the unexpected respite her massage afforded me. However, my blissful moment of peace was short-lived.

"I've been thinking about that new biotech business in Santa Barbara," Red said as she sat up and wrapped the sheet around her.

I shook my index finger at her. "Uh, uh. First of all, you're supposed to be delightfully relaxed after all my work. Secondly, no lobbying. I'm here as a masseuse, not a council member."

"Pshaw. I'm not lobbying; I'm merely letting you know. We've got a group together that's concerned about the poisoning of the environment."

"You mean the squirrel issue in Shoreline Park?"

Red found a pen and jotted something down. "That wasn't on our list, but who knows what's going to happen to all that poison when the rains come." She scratched her temple with the top of the pen. "We're really concerned about the research company," she added as she wrote another note.

"Which one is that?"

"Highland Medical Research and Development. I've heard complaints about their practices. They get away with it because they're supposedly looking for cures for all sorts of terrible diseases, but the chemicals they use are highly toxic, and nobody's watching how they dispose of them. We're going to make sure you people in the council take notice."

"I hate to ask, but who's *we*?"

"MEAP. Montecito Energized Against Pollution. Most of the same group that fought the stupid hotel development plan before the California Coastal Commission. If we can beat down those politically-appointed bureaucratic knuckleheads, you amateurs on the City Council will be a piece of cake."

****

When I got home, I found our cat, Ginger, perched on the edge of our bluff, staring at the beach seventy feet below. I crept up behind her and tried to figure out what caught her feline eye. I spotted Alicia pacing on the sand and misgivings arose in me. Alicia would sometimes stroll the beach with me on a summer evening or take part in a mussel-collecting expedition, but the only time she walked the beach alone was when she was upset. I hoped it didn't mean the police were back after Sarah again.

I hustled down Thousand Steps, three perilous flights of crumbling, goo-covered concrete steps that led from our street to the beach below. When I reached the bottom section, I saw a visibly agitated Alicia headed back toward the stairway.

Our eyes locked, and, when I lifted an eyebrow in question, she said, "I heard from Michelle. She called right after you left for Red's."

I reached for her, and she leaned into my arms. "God, it's

been over four years," I said. "Is she okay?"

Alicia nodded into my chest then drew back. "My beloved sister is in Los Angeles wondering where we are."

I heard the edge in the word "beloved" and figured Michelle was in a momentarily sane, but argumentative, state. "What does she want this time?"

"Somehow it's my fault I left the city without notifying her. Like I knew where she was and could leave a message."

"How did she find you?"

"It's not like we're hiding. All she needed to do is check our names on a computer at the public library. Between the City Council and my real estate business, we're not exactly low profile."

Her voice slid into anger. I persuaded her to climb up the one-hundred-twenty steps to our street and rescue Ginger from her self-imposed vigil.

Alicia's older sister, Michelle, was mentally ill and homeless off and on for the past thirty years. We never knew when she would pop up on our doorstep or when the police would call after picking her up for solicitation or vagrancy.

"You think she's back on her meds?"

Alicia shrugged. "She's on something. Or maybe several somethings. But she has a desire to see her niece and nephew. So, she's taking the Amtrak up here. She'll be here in time for dinner."

My groan was an inward one, or at least I hoped it was. Michelle could be a bright and witty woman, a withdrawn and sullen shrew, or anything in between. It depended on the day and the chemicals whirling through her brain at any moment. Some of the time, those chemicals occurred naturally. Sometimes, they were the result of self-medicating. On good days, physician-prescribed medication helped balance out her moods and lessen her paranoia. For a period of fourteen months, she stayed on her meds and held a job and became a regular part of our lives. Then, one day, four years ago, she walked out on her job, her apartment, and her life. She disappeared, leaving all her belongings for us to pack up and clear out.

"Maybe this time, she'll let us know which shelter she's staying in." I hoped she'd be in a shelter rather than on the streets.

Alicia merely shook her head.

*****

Apprehensive may not be the most comprehensive word to describe my state of mind while awaiting the arrival of the 5:41 p.m. Amtrak train from Los Angeles, but it dominated my body. I didn't know if I wanted Michelle to step off the train or to have changed her mind and disappeared again.

Before I could decide, the bells heralding the approach of the train clanged. Michelle was the third person to descend the steps. She was the same height as Alicia, but her ash blonde hair was streaked with white. The sleeves of her shirt ended an inch above her wrists while her pants dragged a little on the ground. But her clothes looked clean, as did she. She spotted me and held out her arms.

I hugged her and felt more bones than muscle or fat. When I studied her faded blue eyes, I saw warmth and humor in them. I smiled with relief. "Welcome to Santa Barbara. Alicia and the kids will meet us at the house."

"She couldn't get up the courage to face me, huh?" Michelle squeezed my arm then gripped her backpack. We ambled back to the car. "I don't much blame her. There are days I don't know who I'll be when I wake up."

"New meds?" I asked as she clicked her seatbelt closed.

"Yeah. I got hooked up with a doctor when I was in San Diego. He thinks I'm bipolar as well as schitzo. So, I'm trying a new batch of multicolored delights."

A thought flitted by as to how long she'd stay on the regimen. I pushed it away. "Did Allie tell you about the new additions to our family?"

Surprise flickered across Michelle's face. "The kids have been popping babies?"

"Sarah married David, and she gave birth to Amy last year."

Michelle shook her head. "I guess more time has passed than I thought."

The family greeted us when we drove up to the house. The last time Michelle saw Ben and Sarah they were in their teens, but she called them by name and hugged them both. I was pleased when the kids each gave her a long hug in return. She cooed over Amy, but then, who wouldn't? The reunion of the sisters was a bit more restrained.

Michelle cocked her head and examined Alicia. "Damn, you look like the younger sister now more than ever. Don't you ever age?"

Alicia didn't mince words. "And you look like you've been to hell and back."

"I have." Michelle floated her hands over her body. "But at least I made it back from hell, and here I am."

Alicia shook her head before giving Michelle a fierce hug.

Dinner proved a lively affair. The kids provided most of the conversation, although bits and pieces of Michelle's journeys filtered through. Her sojourn in San Diego was preceded by stays in Las Vegas, Portland, and various parts of Arizona. I noted she never mentioned jobs, only brief stories of funny people she'd met along the way.

As Ben cleared the plates, I asked, "How long do you think you'll be in Santa Barbara?"

Michelle shrugged. "At least a couple of months. This place has great weather. And one of the shelters here has a clinic that provides meds." She seemed about to add something, but merely shrugged again.

I glanced at Alicia to see if she was going to extend the offer we discussed. When silence ensued, I dove in. "You know you're welcome to stay with us. Since the kids have sprouted wings, we have two extra bedrooms. You're welcome to one."

"Thanks, but I'm good. In fact, I'll need to leave soon if I'm going to make sure I have a bed over at the shelter."

"Michelle, you really don't have to do that tonight," Alicia said. "It's late. Stay here. You can decide tomorrow if you want to stay with us longer than that."

The sisters exchanged a long look. I couldn't tell what messages were being sent and received, but Michelle must have gotten some reassurance of Alicia's sincerity since she said, "Okay. One night. It'll be nice not having to stand in line for the showers."

Amy started to wail, and Sarah excused herself to take her off for a breastfeeding session while Alicia showed Michelle to Ben's old room.

After the others left the dining room, Ben said, "It's nice to see Aunt Michelle again. She looks pretty good, considering."

"Yeah. Considering."

Chapter **Four**

Monday morning, I rose early and scooted out the door before Alicia or Michelle stirred. An 8:30 a.m. finance committee meeting was scheduled at City Hall and I wanted to get there before it started. City Hall was on a plaza fronting several Spanish Revival-style buildings, including one housing the *Santa Barbara News Press*. I waved at one of the reporters I knew as I climbed the steps into the small, first-floor lobby. Council chambers were on the second floor up a flight of concrete steps. A new, three-person elevator was available, but I preferred the exercise.

Our executive assistant greeted me and buzzed me into the reception area. The offices of the council members and mayor all faced this central area.

"Anybody here?"

"Only the mayor. She's on a conference call."

I thanked her and ducked into my office, which held my desk, a guest chair, two bookshelves, and a tall, three-drawer file cabinet—not spacious, but more than sufficient for the work I did while here. Mostly I worked from home with electronic notifications of meeting agendas and proposals. Occasionally, written communiqués or phone messages came in from my district, so I tried to stop by the office every day.

A labeled, manila folder lay in the middle of my otherwise pristine desk. I slid out the enclosed sheet of paper and casually glanced through it. Dumbfounded, I plopped onto my rolling chair and read the paper more carefully. It detailed a proposal by the mayor to change how the police dealt with any vagrants. My chair creaked as I leaned back and considered this new proposal and all the potential ramifications. Besides the basic inhumanity of the proposal, if it passed, the city might as well hand its treasury over to a lawyer because massive lawsuits were sure to follow. Mayor Julia Thompson hit the trifecta of imprudence, bigotry, and stupidity with this one. The more I thought about it, the angrier I became.

I clutched the proposal and marched into her office. It was larger than the ones for council members, allowing space for a table with four chairs. Paintings done by school children and posters from the annual Solstice Parade covered the walls. In a corner stood a tall, metal sculpture with both smooth and rough surfaces, vaguely in the shape of a tree. I knew it was one of Thompson's works. She earned some acclaim as a local artist.

Thompson looked up. I threw the paper onto her antique oak desk. "Not even you could be serious about this motion to round up all the homeless people in Santa Barbara and bus them to other cities."

"Of course, I am. This is a health and public safety matter. You know as well as I do those unsanitary bums are a danger to everyone. They go stumbling around on the streets, pushing their filthy shopping carts, dropping used needles in the parks, and hassling the tourists who come to spend good money in our city. If you were a mother, you'd realize that. You'd want to protect your children even if you don't care about the economy of this community."

I slapped my hands on her desk and leaned toward her. "First of all, many of those 'bums,' as you call them, are mentally ill. They're not responsible for their actions. Some are addicts, but that doesn't make them any less worthy of services. All of them need to be helped, not herded up and dumped in Goleta." I stood and looked down at her. "And I'll remind you I am a mother, even though that fact has nothing to do with this argument."

Thompson waved away my protests. "You're not really a mother. You didn't give birth or anything."

I stared at her in disbelief for several seconds. "You do know you've insulted every adoptive and stepparent in the world as well as calling into question the parenting status of every father since they didn't give birth to their children." I pointed at a framed photo on her desk. Three dark-haired children and a white poodle surrounded Thompson in a studio portrait. "I'm sure your husband would have a thing or two to say about not being a parent to your children."

"My ex-husband, and he's never been much of a parent to my kids, not that it's any of your business. And none of this has to do with my proposal." Thompson picked up a pen from her desk and pointed it in my face. "First of all, I'm not rounding the homeless up and dumping them. Goleta has several daytime shelters in place. We don't have any. So, we're actually serving them better by transporting them to where they'll get more services and we'll get a tramp-free town. We already move some to a ranch in San Luis Obispo. By all reports, they do quite well up there. This would merely expand the program." She rapped the pen on her desk. "You don't get it. This city will not have any money to do any of your goody-goody social work or any other lefty, liberal, feel-good project you come up with if we don't have a safe place for tourists to visit. No tourists, no money. And keeping tourists coming means no goddamn squirrels ruining our parks and no scary vagrants mumbling to themselves and panhandling on the streets." She ran two fingers over her chest where a red welt showed above the collar of her blouse. "I'd exile those nut-case animal rights people, too, if I could."

"Leaving only the blonde, blue-eyed master race behind. You and Adolf would make a good pair."

****

When I returned home after the finance committee meeting, Alicia was gathering her files and paperwork for her day in her Goleta real estate office. She managed the office, and although seven other agents worked under her, she did her fair share of direct buying and selling with clients.

"Michelle insisted on going to the shelter." Alicia stuffed her notepad computer into her satchel.

I handed her a sweater knowing her office tended to be cool. "Do you know which one she's at?"

"Yes. I drove her over there. I even stayed and watched her go inside." She turned worried eyes in my direction. "Why do I have the feeling I'll never see her again?"

I hugged her close. "Let's go over there tonight and take her out to dinner. See how she's doing."

Alicia gave me a squeeze before releasing me from the embrace. "I know I'm being silly. It's so strange seeing her like this, and yet, in some ways, she's still the sister I've always known. She's even hauling around the copy of *A Tale of Two Cities* I bought her when she went away to college."

"Her favorite book. I remember discussing it with her when we first met."

Alicia gave a sigh. "I feel like we just took one of the kids to kindergarten or something."

"She's a grown woman, and she probably has more street smarts and better coping skills than either of us."

"You're right."

"As always."

"Don't you wish?" Alicia patted my cheek, picked up her purse, and headed for the door. "I'll be back around five. Your delusions can keep you company until then."

****

Sarah's usual babysitter fell through, so she called and asked if I would watch Amy while she went to her job at Earth Ethics. I happily agreed.

After Sarah dropped Amy off, my favorite grandchild and I went out in the backyard so she could play in her shaded playpen. She could roll over and reach for her toys, so I placed several of her favorites near her. She and I discussed each stuffed animal as I tucked them into the enclosure. We played happily together for an hour before the doorbell interrupted us.

I gathered Amy in my arms, went into the house, and opened the front door. A young man with sandy hair and a surfer's tan greeted me.

"I'm John Johnson from the *News Press*." He grabbed a laminated press card that dangled on a lanyard around his neck and held it up at eye level for my viewing pleasure.

"John Johnson?"

He gave a wry grin. "My parents weren't very imaginative. It's actually worse. My full name is John Johnson, Jr."

I bounced Amy in my arms as I considered slamming the door in his face. Good manners prevailed, and I asked, "What is it you want, Mr. Johnson?"

"I was hoping to get your comments on Jeffrey Henderson. As I'm sure you're aware, he was the man who fired a paintball at the council last Tuesday. I was there. Since you were seated right beside the mayor, it's possible the paintball was meant for you. Now, you *just happened* to find Mr. Henderson murdered in a park where you *just happened* to be. So, I thought you might want to tell your side of the story." He raised a recording device.

"No comment."

"What about this? I met with Mr. Henderson a few days ago. He alleged he had evidence of major corruption that led to the highest political offices in the city. Now, the police have found Mr. Henderson's apartment was broken into and searched. Did you find what you were looking for?"

This time good manners lost. I stepped back and closed the door.

I ignored the persistent ringing of the doorbell and headed back outside, glad for the locking gate we installed last year to secure entrance to our backyard. Having to remember to unlock it was a nuisance when people came for a massage in our gazebo, but the sense of security it gave us overrode the annoyance.

I thought about what the reporter insinuated and saw how the *News Press* might twist what happened to make a story where none existed. I imagined how delighted Johnson would be if he knew Sarah had even a loose connection to the case. I considered what I could do about it and concluded nothing could be done except to avoid adding fuel to the fire. A phone call from Sarah interrupted my brooding.

"The police confiscated all of my records here at work. My boss is having a fit over attorney-client privileges, but I'm not an attorney yet, so there's not much they can do."

"Did the search warrant specify anything in particular?"

"It's pretty broad. They want anything to do with Jeffrey Henderson, Animals First, any animal rights groups affiliated with them, or any other groups sympathetic to their causes. Since that's pretty much my entire client base, my files are stripped clear."

"Can't they tell from your business card who made

the appointment?"

Sarah gave an exasperated sigh. "Henderson had the nerve to bleed all over it. Can't read a thing."

I urged caution around the police, and Sarah agreed to say as little as possible. I gathered Amy and her assorted stuffed friends and moved back into the house. Before we could settle ourselves, Ben burst through the front door.

"I might have an internship," he announced from the kitchen where he attacked the contents of the refrigerator in search of a snack. I knew, despite whatever he consumed now, he'd still eat a full dinner. His appetite astounded me.

"Great. Where?"

"Highland Medical Research and Development. They opened a lab here a couple of years ago, and they're starting a new research project to prevent Alzheimer's."

"How strange. Red mentioned the company yesterday." I didn't think it prudent to tell Ben about Red's negative comments concerning his possible future employer.

A glimmer of a memory regarding an article on the company moving to Santa Barbara flickered in my brain. I hoped the difficulty I had remembering the article didn't mean I was going to be needing whatever Alzheimer's cures Highland may come up with. From what I could dredge up from my memory banks, the newspaper piece wasn't glowing. But, then, the owner of the *News Press* tended to be anti-development in any respect. "Sounds like a worthy cause. What will you be doing?"

"It's not for sure yet," Ben said, as he wandered into the living room with two apples, some cheddar cheese, and a roasted chicken leg. "I'm interviewing tomorrow for a lab assistant post. They do a lot of cutting-edge stuff, so I could get great R and D experience."

"Will you still have time to concoct my clients' oils and creams?" Ben was the creator of the specialized lotions I used in my massage business.

He looked hurt. "Do you really need to ask? I wouldn't give it up for the world. But this is a paid internship, and I'll need the money to expand my lab."

Ben shared a rented house on the working-class outskirts of town with two other men. Atypical for the area, the house held a basement. Ben converted it into a lab and production facility. His dream was to create new topical ointments to cure everything from acne to skin cancer, depending on the day. In the meantime, he experimented a lot and he kept me supplied with high-end massage materials individually designed for each of my clients. In return, I bankrolled most of his lab. The situation seemed to meet both our needs.

I bounced Amy on my knee while she chewed on her knuckle. "College and massage oil production will still leave you enough time to take on a job?"

"This is an easy semester. Only one class in pharmacology. The rest are electives. Then it's only one more semester, and I'm out." He chomped down on the chicken leg as if to emphasize the point.

Out and doing what? I wanted to ask, but I held my tongue. Ben was an all-around good kid, and he'd find his way. Sooner, I hoped, rather than later. "Sarah called. The police arrived at her law firm armed with a warrant. Seems they're still centered on the tenuous link of her business card. They flashed the dead man's picture around. No one Sarah talked to had seen him at the office. Looks more and more like someone outside the firm gave him the card."

Ben swallowed before asking, "Why would someone else make an appointment for him? It's not like he's some big celebrity who needs a front man to keep the paparazzi at bay." He cut a slice of apple and balanced a chunk of cheddar on it and offered it to me. When I waved him off, he scarfed it down before asking, "Whose name was on the appointment list?"

"Ah, there's the rub. Jeffrey Henderson bled all over the card. The police were only able to make out most of Sarah's name and some of Earth Ethics'. They identified the company mainly from its logo."

Ben asked, "No CSI magic to reveal the hidden writing?"

"No tech or no funds. Or they don't think it's worth the time and money until they're sure there's a tie-in. Or maybe they're working on it, and it takes more than thirty minutes to do crime lab stuff in real life. In any case, it sounds like it lets Sarah off the hook, at least for the moment."

"I hope not. This is the first time my oh-so-proper sister

has ever had her name linked to public scandal. I'm beginning to like it."

****

"Michelle seemed good. It's amazing she's already gotten a job. Those counselors at the shelter are pretty awesome," I said as I pulled off my shirt and tossed it into the dirty-clothes basket. Dinner with Michelle went well. She seemed pleased to see us and excited about the job opportunity, even though it meant working weekends and some late nights.

Alicia also changed into her nightclothes. She was undressed from the waist up, and her back was to me. I snuck closer and wrapped one arm around her midriff while my other hand swept her hair from her neck. I started nibbling her luscious, long neck when I felt her pat my arm. It was her "thanks, but no thanks" signal. I rested my chin on her shoulder. "Something wrong?"

"Should I have offered her some of the trust fund to set her up in an apartment?" She turned in my arms and snuggled her head against my chest. "It's so hard to know what to do."

Alicia and Michelle's parents weren't well-off, but when they sold their house, they put the money into a trust for both their daughters. Alicia was named as trustee, and they left specific directions for Michelle to be cared for, but she wasn't allowed access to any of the principal of the funds.

It was the "cared for" part that was tricky.

Alicia slipped from my grasp and pulled a night shirt over her head. "We set her up last time. It seemed like it helped her. Gave her her own space. She stayed there for over a year."

"We waited until she'd held a job for a month before arranging for the apartment."

"I know. I know." Alicia collapsed on the side of the bed. "It's just that she looks so good this time. The new medications seem to be working for her. She's reasonable and rational and—" She flung her hand in the air as if in despair.

"Let's give it at least a week," I said. "The shelter is working for her at the moment. Let's see how she does with this cleaning crew job." I flashed a grin. "It actually seems like a good match for her. When she's on her cleanliness jag, there's no equal for her thoroughness."

Alicia patted the bed beside her in invitation. I finished changing and slid under the covers. She laid her head on my shoulder and ran her fingers lightly up and down my sternum. "I love you and your logical, lawyerly mind."

"Not always. You hate it when I'm reasonable and you're being emotional."

"True. But in this case, your Mr. Spock persona is welcome."

I held up my right hand with the ring and middle finger separated in true Vulcan fashion. "Then may we all live long and prosper."

"Right now, I'll settle for living peacefully."

"Agreed. Do you mind if I check in on the news?" Despite my initial protests, we installed a television on the wall of the bedroom. Even though it was originally Alicia's idea, I seemed to be the one to flip it on most of the time. Tonight was no exception.

Gang violence headed the newscast. I took a mental note to speak to the police chief about intervention and prevention programs. We needed to find out what was really working and what wasn't. The name of Highland Medical Research and Development pierced the fog of my musings. I turned up the volume on a prerecorded scene of a small crowd waving signs outside of a streamlined, modern, concrete building.

A small woman with a microphone and impossibly white teeth said, "The picketers are protesting the use of animals in the research of drugs and cosmetics."

The reporter invited a man over to stand beside her. The scroll on the bottom of the screen identified him as Dr. Kyle Hench, director of research and development for Highland Medical. Dr. Hench was telling her of the necessity for testing products, medications, and procedures on live animals to ensure the safety of humans who would be using such items.

My cynical side noted the company picked a photogenic person to be their spokesperson. Hench's dark hair swept over his forehead in an unruly way. His chiseled chin featured the currently popular five o'clock shadow. For some reason, he made me think of a movie version of a hunter or fisherman. The rugged, outdoorsy type, but a little too clean to be real.

The chanting continued even as the police rolled onto the scene. The protest ended peacefully.

"That's where Ben might be working," I said to Alicia.

"Ben's going to work where there's animal testing? The child who won't kill a spider or a fly and hates it when we use lethal methods to get rid of ants in the house?"

"That's the one. Expect the police on our doorstep if there's a mysterious disappearance of all the test subjects in the lab."

Alicia turned over onto her back. "I can see it now. Our son knocking on the door and asking if he can stash a few dozen monkeys in the garage."

"Not Ben. He'd give them his bedroom, and he'd take the garage."

"Oh, Lord. How did we ever raise such socially-conscious kids?"

I turned off the television and kissed her cheek. "They obviously didn't get any of my money-grubbing lawyer DNA, so this one is all on you."

Chapter Five

Ben stood by the kitchen counter when Alicia and I made our way into the kitchen Tuesday morning. His usual sunny demeanor was missing.

"This is an early visit, even for you." I poured him a cup of coffee before asking, "What's up?"

"I got the internship at Highland Medical. I start with them tomorrow." He raked his fingers through his hair.

It was a habit he'd picked up from me. I remember the first time I saw him do it. He was four and having trouble staying in the lines of a coloring book. His gesture and sigh mimicked me so precisely, it made Alicia laugh.

"You don't exactly appear overjoyed. Second thoughts?"

"Nah, nothing like that." He squeezed his hands together before asking, "Ma, would you adopt me?"

If the wall had jumped across the room and whacked into me, I wouldn't feel more dumbfounded. A glance at Alicia told me she was experiencing a similar reaction. I looked at Ben more closely and saw tears shimmering in his eyes. I felt a tear welling in my own. "I'm flabbergasted. And shocked. And honored." I heard myself stumbling over my words. Somewhere my usual eloquence totally deserted me. I tried for a light touch. "I presume this doesn't mean you're disowning your mother."

Ben looked stricken. He turned to Alicia. "I would never do that."

Alicia hugged him. "I know, honey. I think Kate was trying to be funny."

Ben looked relieved. "A friend of mine has two dads. His non-bio dad adopted him as a child. But his bio-mom needed to give up her rights in order for him to adopt. I don't know if that's the case as an adult."

"I have no idea. Family law was not my field. But we can investigate it." I took my turn and hugged Ben tightly then stepped back. "What brought all this on?"

"The paperwork for the job at Highland. They emailed me a packet, and I started in on it last night. They asked for next of kin, and I realized I couldn't list you two as Mom and Ma. It felt weird to write down stepmother for you, and I don't even know if that's the right term. I don't know if we're even legally related to each other." The troubled expression returned to his face.

Strange to hear my own thoughts about Sarah echoed in Ben's words. "You've always been my son, no matter the legalities of it. Since *Obergefell v. Hodges*, our marriage is legal throughout the country and you are officially my step-son. But if you're sure you want to legally become my son, and if your mom's okay with it, I would be so proud to be one of your official mothers."

Alicia wrapped her arms around us both. "It didn't take a piece of paper to make us a couple, and it won't take a piece of paper to make you our son. But if you want paper, we'll make it happen."

****

"He what?" Sarah asked. "Why?"

I was surprised and a little wounded Sarah was not immediately happy about Ben's decision. I became less happy as she continued.

"What about Dad? He's going to be so hurt."

I tensed. Even after more than two decades of mostly non-contact, the thought of Zacharias Wise had that effect on me. "What does this have to do with Zach?"

The question seemed to stop her for a moment.

"Well, he can't have three parents, can he? Wouldn't Dad have to give him up?"

I wanted to say Zacharias gave Ben up at birth, although it wasn't entirely true. Zach was fighting overseas when Ben was born. Alicia and I were friends, and she asked me to be her birthing coach. So, I was the one who held Ben when he was born. I helped Alicia while she dealt with being a single mother to a newborn and a toddler in the intervening months until Zach came home.

Once Zach came back, Alicia's life turned to hell. Zach experienced PTSD and was drinking. He became volatile and verbally abusive. She tolerated it until the day Zach shook baby Ben violently to stop him from crying. Within minutes, Alicia gathered the children and left. She had nothing and nowhere to go. I offered the spare rooms in my condo, and she accepted. It wasn't until three months after Alicia filed for a divorce that our love story began, but facts didn't stop Zach from blaming me for the breakup of his family.

Instead of reviewing this ancient history with Sarah, I took a deep breath and said, "Family law isn't either of our specialties. But I'm willing to bet that, as an adult, Ben can do as he darned well pleases."

****

I was still irritated with Sarah as I took my seat in the council chambers for our Tuesday afternoon meeting. The council chambers filled and threatened to spill out the doors and onto the overflow balcony.

My fellow council member, Sanchez, leaned over and whispered, "Fasten your seatbelt. It's going to be a bumpy ride. I heard both the animal rights activists and the homeless advocates are out in force today."

I spotted John Johnson from the *News Press* standing along the back wall taking notes. His update article on Jeffrey Henderson's murder investigation in the morning paper reported a lack of progress in the case. No suspects or persons of interest were identified. Thankfully, the article didn't include any allegations regarding my involvement, nor did it mention possible political scandals. I hoped it meant he dropped those lines of inquiry.

The only new piece of information in the newspaper article was the suspicion a "ghost gun" might be the murder weapon. A few months back, the police chief and I discussed the dangers of these weapons made from kits. The resulting guns have no serial numbers, and the bullets fired from them don't have the distinctive, and identifiable, grooves a manufactured gun leaves. A drill press and a few metal-working tools are the only things needed to put them together.

These weapons were quickly becoming the scourge of law enforcement.

I took out my notepad and turned my attention to the vast number of speakers clamoring to be heard. Although speakers were limited to three minutes each for non-agendized items, the public-address portion of the meeting took over an hour. Advocates for animal rights and the homeless vied with store owners and park preservationists. The only thing they all agreed upon was the City Council wasn't doing anything right.

A woman wearing an "Animals First!" T-shirt identified herself as a Marine Corps veteran. She provided a scathing review of the city's ground squirrel population control program. She cited evidence showing the program not only accidentally poisoned other animals, but also did irreparable damage to the environment through the poison's effect on everything from microorganisms to the ground water.

I noticed the mayor shifting in her seat. I wondered how much more criticism she could take of the plan before she banged the gavel and postponed the rest of the public input portion of the meeting until after the agenda items were completed. Then I saw my daughter step to the mike.

After giving her name and address, Sarah said, "I'm here to give voice to the voiceless." Her eloquent speech touched on both the animals affected by the poison in the park and the homeless who were "ill-cared for, if not openly abused" by the city. Applause greeted her remarks. She lifted an eyebrow at me before she sat down.

I recognized the challenge in that look. She flung it at me often enough when we debated issues and she felt she produced the winning argument. I could envision her championing causes, speaking at rallies, organizing the troops with a clarion call to arms. God forbid, I could even see her running for office. Of our two children, she was the most like me, and yet, she was her own strongly opinionated woman. I smiled.

The mayor's response was not as warm and fuzzy. Thompson glared at me as the next speaker introduced himself. I considered reminding her that since she didn't consider Sarah to be my daughter, she shouldn't be blaming me for her actions, but I remembered this would be expecting rationality from an irrational source. Instead, I busied myself with taking notes on the speaker's views.

By the time we reached Thompson's agenda item on the relocation of vagrants, meeting fatigue appeared to have set in for most of the council if not all the attendees. Civility was becoming a rare commodity.

Sanchez's hand shot up as soon as Thompson opened the motion to discussion after accepting a second from a council member whose sixth district included the downtown business areas.

Sanchez leaned forward, clasped his hands together, and stared at Thompson. "Madame Mayor, while I absolutely support improving both the safety of our city and the social services we offer to the more unfortunate inhabitants of our city, I do not consider deporting people a practical or humane solution. People come from all over the world to visit Santa Barbara. Should we start giving everyone a fiscal test before allowing them to enter our city to ensure they will not become dependent on the city for social or medical services? Is the next thing a border wall at the city limits so the ones we bus out of town can't return?"

Thompson's face reddened as she studiously stared at her agenda notes. At least some of Sanchez's points seemed to be piercing her rather thin skin.

Apparently unable to catch Thompson's eye for a direct confrontation, Sanchez turned to the citizens in the council chambers, addressing them instead. "The police state is coming, folks. You think it might not matter if we rid our city of a few 'undesirable' people. That this might even make life better. But who are the ones who get to decide which person is undesirable? Today it's someone sleeping on a sidewalk. Tomorrow it may be the surfers who endanger the swimmers at the beach. Then maybe the smaller shops with unique trinkets someone else deems tacky. And, hey, what about all those older people who crowd up our streets with slow driving and overtax our hospitals with their illnesses? Why not have an upper age limit on residents? And don't get me started on Muslims and Jews."

Thompson slammed her gavel. "Mr. Sanchez, either stick

to the motion at hand or cede your turn. This ridiculous harangue of yours has gone on long enough."

Before outright civil war could erupt, I raised my hand. "I move to table this proposal."

Thompson's fury swung to me. "We're not going to table this. We're going to discuss this and get this in action."

"Uh, Madam Mayor." The sixth district representative cleared his throat. "A point of order. A motion to table must be voted on with no discussion."

I thought Thompson was going to pound her gavel on the poor man's fingers, but she gained control and called for the vote. The motion to table won four to three.

After the meeting, Sanchez yanked my sleeve and pulled me off to one side. "Why did you move to table that? You saw the vote. We could have killed that monstrosity tonight."

"Maybe. But two of those votes to table came from Thompson's buddies. I think they want to duck for cover without directly opposing the all-powerful Oz."

Sanchez's face relaxed from an angry scowl to a thoughtful gaze. After several seconds of silence, he said, "And a week's worth of publicity on the subject might have some impact on their little political souls as well."

I agreed to a point. "Right now, districts three and six might have trouble voting against all the business interests in their areas. I don't know whether newspaper coverage is going to change that, but we can hope. We need one and four to swing our way. And the *News Press* has good reach in those districts."

"That's great. But another hot spot is erupting. I got word more protests are planned for Shoreline Park next week over the ground squirrel fiasco. I thought it might be a good way to get public opinion on our side, but then I heard there's going to be counter-protestors there."

"There are going to be people there who are *for* killing ground squirrels?" I tried to picture those protest signs.

"Not so much. I heard that it's a group of skinheads and other neo-Nazi groups from outside the city who are going around disrupting any protests they deem liberal, progressive, or anti-white male. It could get nasty."

"In that case, even our dear mayor may think it's a good

idea to put this to rest before Santa Barbara gets that kind of publicity."

"Maybe. But we'd need to come up with a solution and the city manager's support for it before next Tuesday."

I scanned my notes on the people and organizations who spoke at the City Council meeting, searching for someone who could conceivably have concrete ideas on how to handle the problem. "I've got an idea. Let me check into it and get back to you." I glanced over at the dais where Thompson was huddled with her staff. She shot me a venomous look. I jerked my head in her direction. "I think I've made an enemy of our fair mayor."

"How refreshingly naïve of you, Chica. Your head's been in her crosshairs since you joined this council. And believe me, when she decides to shoot, it isn't going to be with any kiddie-toy paintball popper."

Chapter Six

"You're a City Council member." The raven-haired woman who opened the door of the Animals First offices limped to her desk and seated herself on the far side. She leaned back in the swivel chair and rocked slightly. Her ebony eyes regarded me with an air akin to a scientist studying an insect. She added nothing to her first comment, nor did she offer me a seat.

Undeterred, I sat. I recognized her from the council meeting. She was the one who spoke about the environmental side effects the poisoning program was causing. "Yes. You gave a speech at the meeting today."

"For all the good it did."

I admitted to not remembering her name.

"Sophia Carlotti."

"Wow," I said. "Can't get much more Italian than that."

"If you don't count my Guatemalan mother. But I don't think you're here about my DNA."

Recognizing that charm and conviviality were not going to make inroads with Ms. Carlotti, I decided on a more direct course. "I'm here because your group has made allegations about the damage the city's park program is doing. In fact, one of your members was so angry with what's happening, he shot the mayor."

Carlotti waived her hand in dismissal. "Jeff acted on his own. Animals First didn't aid or abet him in any way. I already made that clear to the police."

"Do you know why he went after the mayor?"

Carlotti shrugged. "Give me a few seconds, and I'm sure I could come up with a dozen reasons."

"How about one?"

"Okay. How about the fact that Julia Thompson is a pompous ass who doesn't care about the environment or animals? Shit, she doesn't even care about other people. Of course, that one I understand."

"People aren't a top priority to you?"

Carlotti leaned farther back in her chair and threw her left leg on the desktop. She yanked up her pants leg to expose a metallic and plastic mechanism where her calf should have been. "Blown off in Afghanistan. I've seen what people can do. What people willingly and stupidly decide to do to each other so they can plant a flag on a piece of land or declare that their god is the right one. Stupid fucking idiots." She dropped her leg with a thunk. "It's one thing when we supposedly superior homo sapiens decide to take each other out. But when we declare war on animals because we don't like where they live or we decide their lives are less important than ours, so we have the right to mutilate and maim in the name of science..." An angry expulsion of air completed her thought.

"Scientists are the ones who developed that prosthesis."

"And do you know how they did that? By chopping perfectly good legs off of hundreds, if not thousands, of monkeys and implanting chips in various parts of their brains. Willingly mutilating animals and then torturing them with brain surgery. That's as bad as the masses of animals that are massacred in the wars. No one ever mentions the livestock and pets that are shot or blown to bits in the Middle East and Afghanistan. You think civilian casualties are underreported? No one even bothers to keep track of the domesticated or wild animals that are part of that carnage."

The anger radiating from Sophia Carlotti was almost palpable. If it had been she, instead of Jeffrey Henderson, in the council chambers, I don't think she would have settled for a paintball gun. I decided to change the subject. "How did you get involved with Animals First?"

"I'm not involved with Animals First. I run it."

"Oh." It was the best I could do. My surprise must have been evident.

Carlotti raised an eyebrow. "You're wondering how an obvious basket case was chosen to manage the organization? That's easy. It's my organization. I founded it. When I got discharged from the Corps, I moved back home and decided to do something to heal the world rather than destroy it.

Figured if people paid attention to helping animals, they'd realize that the bad stuff we're doing to animals is a reflection of what we do to each other. Maybe they'd stop." She shrugged. "Maybe not."

"How active was Jeffrey Henderson in the organization?"

"Jeff recruited new members. He organized a lot of the protests. He also tried to make contact with other groups to see how we could work together. Jeff was much better with people than I am."

The fact Carlotti thought a guy who threatened people with a gun exemplified a people-person told me a lot about her. "Sounds like you and he were friends. I'm sorry for your loss."

"Jeff was a good guy. He's not the first good guy I've known who was killed. The way the world is going, he won't be the last."

"Did Jeff ever try to work directly with any of the City Council members on the ground squirrel issue?"

"Yep. He went straight to the top. Jeff thought working with the system might be better than only protesting. But your charming mayor stonewalled him for three weeks. When she finally gave Jeff five minutes of her precious time, she cut him off before he could even present our ideas. She shoved Jeff out the door then bowed and scraped as she ushered in a bozo who runs a big business in town."

"I'm sorry he didn't reach out to me." I ignored the rude noise Carlotti made in response. "I'm here because I'm interested in any ideas Animals First has about how to deal with the ground squirrels."

Carlotti pushed back from her desk and swirled her chair around to face one of three gunmetal-grey, six-drawer filing cabinets that had seen better days. She pulled a three-inch-wide file out of a drawer and rolled her chair back to her desk. She plopped the thick file in front of me. "Research data on ground squirrels, their place in the environment, a run-down on the effectiveness of nonlethal methods to relocate them, and the consequences for each of these methods, both economic and environmental."

"I'm beyond impressed. Do you have some time now to go through this with me?"

Carlotti raised an eyebrow, as if doubting my sincerity. But she opened the folder and started explaining its contents.

By the time she flipped the manila file folder closed, I gained several practical ideas for how the city manager might approach the problem along with a new appreciation for those industrious (and destructive) little animals.

After thanking Carlotti for the education, I asked, "By the way, you said the mayor cut her meeting with Jeff short so that she could meet with some businessman. Did Jeff know who that was?"

"Jeff knew him, all right. It was Mr. Smooth Talker, Kyle Hench. The doctor from Highland Research. I wish Jeff could have eavesdropped on that conversation. We've been trying to get the goods on that company for over a year."

Chapter Seven

I checked the time then stared at the doorway of the Leafy Greens restaurant once more. It was 8:20 p.m., and Michelle was supposed to meet us for dinner at 8:00. She had insisted that we not pick her up from the shelter. She told us the restaurant was on her way home from her cleaning job and she would meet us here. On time. Twenty minutes ago.

"Maybe she's putting in some overtime. You know, new kid on the block. Only her second day. Least seniority gets stuck doing the extra jobs. Or maybe she thinks this is too much. I mean, dinner two times in a week." I was blabbering away in an effort to relieve Alicia's anxiety. I didn't have to see her face to know unease was creeping over her. I felt it radiating from her body.

"Let's order," Alicia said as she opened the menu once again. "If she isn't here by the time we finish dinner, we'll go over to the shelter."

To start searching for her were the unsaid words. She waved the waiter over, and we placed our orders.

Dinner was a quick and silent affair. I kept darting glances at my watch while Alicia stared at the doorway. We paid and were in our car by a quarter to nine.

The managers of the shelter expressed sympathy but refused to release information about whether or not Michelle was at the shelter, had ever been at the shelter, or where she might be right now. They did encourage us to leave a note for her that they would pin on the message board.

I watched as Alicia wavered between tears and fury. Unable to alleviate her fears, I opted for action. A few women sat on the patio outside the shelter, despite the cool, autumn night air. I approached one and showed her a picture of Michelle. I asked if she knew where Michelle worked. She didn't but pointed me to others who might. It took ten minutes of being shuffled from person to person before I found an older man who thought she got a job through a cleaning agency on Patterson.

I Googled the company name and got the phone number. The call went unanswered. Not unexpected for that time of night but disappointing nonetheless. We returned to our car and slumped in the seats.

I grasped Alicia's hand. "There's not much more we can do tonight. Tomorrow I can call the cleaning company and the police and start checking the other shelters." I was familiar with the shelters in the Los Angeles area, having done several tours through them in previous searches for my sister-in-law. But I was fuzzy about how many shelters there might be in the Santa Barbara area.

"You know the police won't do anything."

"I know they won't go looking for her without evidence of her being kidnapped or in some sort of danger. But we should still fill out a missing person report so they know to keep an eye out for her. They could tell us if she was in an accident or if they picked her up for some reason."

"Like drugs or prostitution?" Alicia's voice was bitter.

"Or loitering. Even without our dear mayor's proposal, the police sometimes roust the homeless when they're blocking access to public places or making a nuisance of themselves."

"And if she's off her meds, God only knows where she could be or what she could be doing."

****

After a fitful night's sleep, we hit the phones at eight the next morning. The Premier Cleaning Services informed us that Michelle clocked in for her job at 10:00 a.m. yesterday but hadn't returned to the company to clock out before it closed at 8:00. They wouldn't disclose where she cleaned, but assured us they would check with that client and let us know what they found out.

The police hadn't picked her up. We filed an official missing person report with the records personnel who reassured us they would pass the information to the watch commander. Calls to the local hospitals yielded no admissions for Michelle. Requests for information from the three other homeless shelters in the city were politely stonewalled. We left messages.

An hour later, we held no leads and fewer options.

"It makes no sense," I said. "It takes time for her meds to wear off. Last time, we could tell she stopped taking them well in advance of her—"

"Her going off her head? Yeah. How rude of her not to give us advance warning."

The fine lines around Alicia's eyes appeared more deeply etched this morning, and her face bore a defeated look. I couldn't watch her slide into deeper despair. "This time, we're not going to wait for Michelle to appear again. I'm going to call my old law firm. I think the detective agency we used has a Santa Barbara branch."

****

"The first time was when Michelle was twenty-two," Alicia told Keesha Collins, a private investigator with Scott and Associates.

The private investigations firm my law firm used didn't have a Central Coast office, but it recommended Scott and Associates. I called and the company said they'd send out one of their investigators within the hour. True to their word, Keesha Collins rang our doorbell a mere forty minutes later.

Collins looked to be in her forties with silver showing in her kinky black hair. Her dark eyes carefully surveyed our living room and both of us before sitting on the loveseat. She asked for Michelle's history and took notes on all that Alicia said.

"My sister is seven years older than me, so I was only fifteen when she disappeared. She was at UCLA double majoring in chemistry and math, pulling A's in every class. Then, with one semester left, she vanished. She finished her fall finals, went back to her dorm room, snatched her purse, and left." Alicia rubbed her face with both hands before continuing. "A few days later, when she didn't come home for winter break, my parents went wild. They called all her friends, but no one knew where she'd gone. We went to her dorm room. Everything was still there. All her clothes, her books, her personal belongings. No one at the dorm could give us a clue what happened to her."

Alicia's face showed the strain of reliving her sister's disappearance. I moved closer and held her hand. She gave my fingers a squeeze and took a deep breath.

"My parents called the police. They were polite, but Michelle was legally an adult, so they were limited in what they could do unless evidence of a crime cropped up. So, my parents hired a private investigator." She looked at Collins as if comparing her to that detective of long ago. "It took him nine weeks to find her trail. She'd taken a bus to Boston then somehow got herself to a coastal town in Maine where she worked flipping hamburgers. When we flew out to get her, she refused to come home. Said *they* were after her in California and she would only be safe on the East Coast."

Alicia leaned back against the couch cushions. "My parents finally persuaded her to be seen by a doctor who diagnosed her as schizophrenic and prescribed some drugs. Once she was on them, she calmed down and came home with us. That was the beginning of the cycling. As long as she was on the meds, she was fine. After a period of feeling fine, she'd decide she no longer needed the meds and she'd go off them. Then she'd slide into depression and paranoia and, sometimes, run away again."

Collins rapidly jotted notes in her notebook. She glanced up when Alicia drew to a stop. "I'll need a list of any places you know your sister stayed during the times she's gone missing." Alicia nodded and Collins asked, "Did Michelle mention anything during this latest visit about friends or contacts or work or shelters that she'd been in recently?"

I answered that one. "She told me she'd been in a shelter in San Diego where she got treatment. Then she was in a different shelter in L.A. for a few weeks while she looked for us. She said she intended to stay in Santa Barbara now. She refused to stay with us. Said there were plenty of nice shelters in Santa Barbara and that she might even camp at the beach for a while."

"But no mention of friends in the area or elsewhere?"

Alicia and I both shook our heads.

Collins stood. "I'll take this photo of Michelle and hit the homeless shelters. I know you've been there, but I'll be talking to the residents, not the staff. Sometimes you get more that way. No privacy rights to worry about." She handed business cards to both of us. "Email me the list of places she's been and any medical information you can remember, especially the names of the new drugs she was taking. I'll be in touch as soon as I have something for you."

I showed Collins to the door then turned to Alicia. Watching the woman I loved in such pain gave me second thoughts about searching for Michelle. "Are you sure you want to go through this again?"

Alicia spent several moments staring out the picture window at the surging waves before replying. "Even as a kid, Michelle experienced these mood swings. I fluctuated between being angry with her, jealous of the attention she got, and being protective of her. When I was eighteen and about to go to college, Michelle was home again, but on the edge. I saw how anxious my parents were, so I told them not to worry, that I would always be there to take care of my sister." She grimaced. "I haven't done a very good job of it up to now. I've got to at least try."

The ring of her cell phone cut into our talk. I heard Ben's voice even before Alicia switched the call to speaker phone.

"I want you to know I'm all right."

Alicia shot me a quizzical glance before asking, "Why shouldn't you be all right?"

"I guess you haven't heard the news. You might want to check online or the local TV channel or even the radio. They're all here. But I have to go now. The police want everyone in the conference room. Gotta go."

I clicked the remote and flipped to our local station. The backdrop was the outside of the Highland Medical Research and Development building, but there were no chanting protestors this time. Instead, the same toothy reporter assumed a grim expression as she recapped what must have run for the last several minutes, if not hours.

"In a gruesome twist to the protests that have plagued Highland Medical for several days now, a cancer researcher was murdered last night."

Chapter Eight

The reporter continued. "The scientist was shot sometime between the hours of five last night and seven this morning. The identity of the victim is being withheld until his next of kin is notified. Reports are that the intruder bizarrely stole some of the lab animals. The police are looking for clues to this mystery."

The station switched to a clip of our local police chief spouting the usual platitudes meant to reassure the public while not divulging any information that would screw up a future legal case. I tuned him out in less than ten seconds. I turned to Alicia. "If it's an animal rights advocate, why would they steal some of the animals and leave the others in the lab? Why not free them entirely?"

"It sounds like you're more worried about the animals than the poor guy who got shot. That could have been Ben."

Her comment caught me off guard. I'd categorized the research scientist as just that, a scientist and nothing more. I robbed him of his humanity. "You're right. I hadn't thought about it that way. I jumped to motive. The question of why someone would act that way. I skipped the feeling part."

Alicia slumped low on the couch, her fingers tracing the ridges of the textured arm. "Now I'm going to worry about Ben as well as Michelle."

"At least Sarah and Amy are okay."

"And David, too." Alicia tilted her head. "When are you going to warm up to our son-in-law?"

"When he stops glowering at me whenever we meet. Luckily, that happens infrequently since he avoids me whenever possible."

"Give it time, honey. He's been through a lot, and he needs someone to blame."

Oh goody, I thought. I just happen to be the lucky person. "I think we have enough on our plates without adding David to it. If we're going to spend our morning worrying about our family, we might want to prioritize."

"It just so happens I can worry about a million things equally and at the same time. It's not my fault you aren't as multitalented."

The faint smile she gave me reassured me that her sense of humor was resurfacing. I drew her up from the couch. "We're going to get through this. Keesha seems like a capable investigator, and we know Michelle has survived for years on the streets without us. So, if it takes a while to find her, chances are she's okay."

Alicia's eyes clouded over again. "There's one thing I didn't tell you. I helped Michelle repack her things before she went to the shelter. A handgun was tucked under her shirts. When I asked her about it, she told me that the world can be a dangerous place, but she knows how to take care of herself. I didn't see any bullets. I don't know if the thing was loaded or if it was for show, and she didn't want to discuss the matter."

My mind raced through the implications of a mentally unstable person toting a gun through the streets of Santa Barbara. After all, what if Jeffrey Henderson used a revolver rather than a paintball gun? And what if Michelle got angry or scared when a police officer tried to arrest her? Then again, what if one of the homeless men tried to attack her? I shook my head. "Scary as the thought is, I'm not sure what we can do about it until Keesha finds her."

"Maybe we ought to warn Keesha?"

"Good idea." I reached for the phone.

"Thanks for the heads up," Collins replied after I told her of the gun. "No one's mentioned seeing her armed, but I'll keep it in mind as I go. I've confirmed that Michelle checked in on time to her work yesterday morning. The others on her shift verify that she was cleaning her assigned section. Her supervisor said the last she saw of Michelle was when she started the last wing of her section. The supervisor left that building to check on another crew. The other crew members left the building and returned to the office at 7:30. None of them remember seeing Michelle at that point. But they didn't think much of it because sometimes one or another of the workers takes a little longer when the rooms need more attention."

I considered the logistics. "Isn't it strange to have a cleaning crew come in during the day? Don't most businesses want their offices cleaned at night when they won't disturb the employees?"

"I asked about that. It's a seven-day-a-week, high-security firm, but most workers are gone by five during the week and by noon on the weekends. They have a cleaning crew come through in the late afternoons to clean the hallways and reception areas."

"Unsupervised by the supposedly security-minded company?"

"Evidently. But the cleaning firm maintains its employees do not have access to any of the secured portions of the company."

"What company is this?"

"Highland Medical."

After hanging up, I reported the conversation to Alicia. I could tell she wasn't taking it well. "Honey, there's no evidence that Michelle was anywhere near that lab where the guy was shot," I said. "Besides, how likely is it that she'd be carrying her gun to work?"

Alicia silently rearranged the magazines on the coffee table. For the third time in the last four minutes. My heart ached for her, but I was unsure what, if anything, could lift her worry. I plunged on anyway. "There are sure to be security cameras. The police would be pounding on the door if Michelle was shown wandering places she shouldn't have been."

"Maybe," Alicia said. "And maybe the police don't know who she is. Or maybe that scientist wasn't the only one to be murdered last night."

I saw pain flicker over her face and rushed to reassure her. "If anything bad happened to Michelle, there would be signs. The police would have noticed."

"If she wasn't killed and she didn't shoot the guy, where is she? Why didn't she check in after work? Why didn't she meet us for dinner?"

I wished I could answer even one of those questions.

As it happened, the police were not far behind. Within

two hours, a knock sounded on the door. Detectives Levine and Ruiz, the same two officers who questioned Sarah about Jeffrey Henderson's death, were once again seated on our living room couch. After fencing about their reasons for their questions, they admitted they were investigating the murder at the Highland pharmaceutical lab.

"Why are you asking about my sister?"

I saw the stern set of Alicia's jaw and noted her crossed arms. Clearly, she was not going to cooperate without a battle. I settled farther back in my chair and watched the detectives.

Ruiz spoke first. "Ma'am, we're checking with everyone who was at Highland Medical yesterday. All we want to do is ask your sister a few questions. Are you sure you have no idea where she is?"

"If we did, would we have called the police this morning to see if they knew anything about her? Would we have filed a missing person report? Would we have called every hospital in the area?"

"And you say she disappears frequently?"

Alicia narrowed her eyes. "Michelle has challenges. She's been homeless for most of the last thirty years. Sometimes we don't hear from her for years at a time."

Detective Levine asked, "Has she ever been known to be violent?"

Alicia shook her head no.

"Do you know how she reacts to surprises? If, maybe, somebody acted inappropriately or scared her?" Ruiz raised his eyebrows.

Alicia uncrossed her arms and leaned forward. "None of us may ever hear from her again."

Chapter Nine

As the police detectives exited, the phone rang. Alicia leapt across the room and grabbed it before our answering system kicked in. Her face fell and she handed the phone to me.

Sean Gregory, the manager of our local animal shelter was on the line. "Kate, I know you're a big supporter of the Humane Society, which is why I'm calling."

Despite my regard for Sean, I was in no mood for social chitchat and my voice reflected my impatience. "What can I do for you, Sean?"

"We've got a bit of a problem here. When the staff opened this morning, there were four large crates filled with monkeys, rabbits, and rats in our drop-off area. The staff checked them out, and most were in poor shape. They're being given IV fluids and fed."

I waited a beat, but Sean remained silent. "If you're looking for foster homes, I'm not in any position to take in—"

"No, no. It's a political problem. That's why I called you. You see, the crates belong to Highland Medical."

It was my turn to be silent for a moment. "You think they might be the animals taken during the break-in? If that's true, this is a legal matter, not a political one."

"It may be both because, frankly, given the shape they're in, I can't see returning those animals to that company."

I glanced at Alicia, hating to leave her with the whole uproar of Michelle going on. But she waved her hand to shoo me away. "Call the police. Then call Highland. I'm on my way."

****

I've never understood how protestors find out there's something to be upset about before the news even hits any news outlets. Is there a subgroup on Meet Up for protestors? I suppose there must be some electronic underground to spread the information, because in the twenty minutes it took me to reach the animal shelter on Overpass Road, a dozen people stood in front of the Humane Society waving signs protesting animal abuse by Highland Medical. Three police officers tried to contain them. I spotted Johnson from the *News Press*, recording device in hand, interviewing the protestors.

I showed my driver's license to one of the officers who waved me through. Sean unlocked the door and ushered me in. Detectives Levine and Ruiz were both toward the end of a long hallway with a group of crime scene investigators. The detectives didn't acknowledge my presence, so I felt free to ignore them as well.

Sean slumped into his desk chair. "I did like you suggested and called Highland. They're sending one of their people over to inspect the crates and the animals. He should be here soon."

"And if the animals belong to them?"

"That's where friends in high places come in. Namely you."

"Sean, come on. If these animals were stolen from Highland, they have a right to get them back."

"Even if they were torturing them? We remove animals from abusive environments all the time. We have a duty to do that. If we see someone abusing an animal on the street, we can take that animal from them right then. If someone leaves their dog in a car with the windows up, we are mandated to break the window and take the dog back here. Is this really any different?"

A rich, deep voice from behind me answered, "It certainly is. Those animals are the property of Highland Medical Research and Development and they are priceless experiments that are leading to a cure for lymphoma. They're not being mistreated."

I glanced up and recognized the spokesperson for Highland whom I'd seen on television. I couldn't remember his name, but the slight growth on his cheeks and his rugged good looks were memorable. However, this time he looked less like a movie actor. That could be because he was glaring at Sean rather than smiling into a camera.

Sean scowled back. "I think we'll have to let our lawyers and the City Council weigh in on that, whoever you are."

"Dr. Kyle Hench. Here's my card. You can call the corporate office to confirm I have the authority to reclaim all our property."

"They're not property. They're animals that depend on us for their welfare."

I intervened. "Don't you have a video camera covering the drop-off area?"

"For all the good it does us." Sean flipped his computer screen around to face us.

The image flickered and then a figure appeared, unloading crates from an off-camera car.

"The camera didn't catch the car let alone the license plate."

The figure moved into a lighted area of the parking lot, not that it helped. The person was dressed like a ninja, all in black, complete with gloves, hood, and face mask. The only recognizable characteristics were that the person was slender and medium height, smallish for a man, above average for a woman, but the sex of the individual was impossible to determine.

"Someone didn't want to be recognized," I said, considering the amount of preparation that must have gone into arranging to drop the animals off incognito. Was that the murderer of the scientist or an accomplice? The video was both tantalizing and frustrating.

Kyle Hench broke into my thoughts. "There's no time for nonsense. I've got a van out back. You need to pack up our test subjects and get them out there now."

Sean crossed his arms. "That's not going to happen."

"Of course, it is. I need to get those animals to the lab so we can get them back on their medication and testing schedules."

Sean raised an eyebrow. "Over my dead body."

****

With no power to intervene on either side, I left the two

men to their stare-down and hurried home to find Alicia gazing out our front windows at the restless ocean. I doubted she saw any whitecaps, pelicans, or even the dolphins that surfed the waves. In the twenty-five years I'd known Alicia, she'd never gone catatonic, but I sensed she was close. I wracked my brain for some action we could take to pull her out of her depression.

"Hey, listen," I said, squeezing her hand. "A reporter once told me about an abandoned building in town that's sometimes a homeless hangout. We haven't looked there, and I didn't think to mention it to Keesha. Why don't we check it out?"

Alicia sighed deeply. "Anything is better than sitting here waiting for the rest of the sky to fall."

I pulled Alicia up from the couch and fished my car keys from the bowl by the front door. We started out for the south side of town.

A large industrial park comprised a major section of East Gutierrez Street. The tan buildings looked like what they were: warehouses. Light industries, auto glass shops, flooring wholesalers, and miscellaneous small businesses filled most of the complexes. A "For Sale" sign stood in front of one of the buildings at the end of the block. The face of that building was freshly painted, all the windows were intact, and the small patch of yard was weed-free, but there were seven men and women sitting on that tiny yard. Shopping carts filled with personal belongings and lumpy sacks sat beside them.

We drove past the warehouse, trying to see if the door to the building was broken. The dark recess of the doorway made it difficult to tell. I parked and we hiked back to the group in front.

My greeting yielded several curious yet wary looks. I think they regarded us with less trepidation than we them, perhaps because they outnumbered us. Two of the women met my eyes. The other two muttered to themselves and looked off toward whatever fascinating scene was occurring across the street or in their minds. Of the three men, one with colorful tattoos running down both arms glared at me. The other two ignored my existence. Overall, the group was cleaner and friendlier than others I encountered in previous searches for my sister-in-law.

Alicia showed a photo of Michelle to the ones who interacted with us. All we got were head shakes. Then one of the men who had ignored us at the beginning reached out for the picture.

He stiffened when he examined the photo. Then he sniffed and rocked some more. "What do you want with Shelly?"

It wasn't a nickname for Michelle that I knew. I shot a quick glance at Alicia and saw she looked equally puzzled. Then again, we hadn't mentioned any name at all when Alicia gave out the photo, so perhaps we were talking about the same person. The photo certainly evoked a response from the man.

I explained about our relationship to her and how our family was worried about her.

"Guess it's hard for a family not knowing." He handed the photo back to Alicia. "Are you sure she's in Santa Barbara? Haven't seen her here."

Alicia answered. "She stayed with us her first night in town. And we ate dinner with her after that. But then she...disappeared."

The man gave a solemn stare. "If I see her, I'll let her know you're looking for her. Does she have your number?"

I pulled out one of my massage business cards with my cell phone on it. Alicia did the same with her real estate card. "She may not know the home phone number and our cells by heart. This has both. She can reach us anytime on our cell phones. You can, too."

He tucked them into the breast pocket of his green-and-brown-checked shirt that, although old and worn, was somewhat clean.

"What's your name, sir?" I asked, holding out my hand.

He studied my hand for a few seconds before he reached out and shook it. "Sir?" He chuckled. "Haven't heard that title since I got out of the Corps. Call me Lefty."

"Thank you, Lefty. We really appreciate your help. How about if we buy you all some lunch? I saw a diner not far from here. We could pick up some sandwiches for you."

The offer of food awakened more interest. After the

group gave me their requests, I asked Lefty if they were living in the empty warehouse.

"Nope. It's locked up tight, and they have security come around every night. But they're all right guys who let us sleep next to the building for some cover."

As we drove to the diner to place their lunch orders, I felt more hopeful. Not only did I think Lefty would fulfill his promise, but he'd given me a glimmer of an idea of how to thwart Mayor Thompson's detention center plan.

Chapter Ten

Thursday morning, the uproar over the murder at Highland Medical still topped the news. When I got up, I found Alicia flipping through news channels searching for any new information or any hint of suspects in the case. The latest report identified the victim as Dr. Nathan Sloan, but no hint of motive for the crime surfaced.

The ring of our landline phone interrupted my trek to the kitchen for coffee. I didn't recognize the number, but I answered anyway.

"I hear you're looking for me. Stop."

"Michelle?" I punched the speaker button and waved Alicia to my side. "We're both on now. Where are you?"

"I'm fine. Stop looking for me. You'll lead them to me. Stop. Just stop."

The phone went dead. I noted the number and pushed redial. No answer and no voice mail. I figured it was probably a pay phone, rare as those were. I called Collins with the information. She promised to get back to me.

When I hung up from Collins, Alicia and I stared at each other.

Alicia broke the silence. "She must have gotten one of our messages. But which one?"

"The shelter won't tell us if she picked up our note." I knew from experience that shelters not only did not disclose who was or wasn't staying with them, but they also were mum on who did or didn't receive messages. I knew they adhered to privacy laws and protected their charges, but their fidelity to their clients was a royal pain to those of us in search of loved ones. "I wonder if Lefty saw her and gave her our cards."

"I guess it doesn't matter how she got the message. She's obviously off her medications. Paranoid. Secretive." She rubbed her arms as if trying to warm herself. "But how did that happen so fast?"

"She's never called us before to warn us to back off. Maybe this is a weird side effect from one of her new meds?"

"Or maybe she's really in hiding. Maybe she did see something Tuesday night that freaked her out." Alicia pointed to the television where the news report displayed the headline, "Bloodbath at Research Center."

I could imagine what the reporters were saying. I'd heard a lurid description on the radio of the blood-sprayed room with animals screaming and one human body strewn across the floor.

Alicia pointed at the television screen again. "Can you picture what it would do to someone in her condition if she opened the door and saw the gory mess in the lab? Shit. If I saw that, I may have disappeared, too."

I hoped the explanation was that benign. But the image of Michelle with a gun created shards of doubt that shredded my wishful thinking.

****

Keesha Collins called two hours later. "I've got some news on Michelle." Alicia and I were both glued to the phone, awaiting Collins's information.

"The telephone number was a pay phone off State Street. It's in front of a liquor store," Collins said. "The cashier noticed a woman who might be Michelle hanging around the front of the store. Since she didn't enter, he didn't pay much attention. He did say he thought the woman was too clean to be one of the homeless, but she did have a day pack with her that sounded like the one you described."

Alicia broke in. "I guess Michelle might have returned to the shelter to pick up her stuff. That would explain where she found our note to call us."

Collins made a noncommittal sound. "I finally convinced the store owner to let me see the surveillance tape from today. They've experienced problems with vandals, so they have a security camera that films the front of the store. Grainy and indistinct, but the woman in the tape used the phone at the time the call came in to you. She then turned north onto State

Street. There's a bus stop on the street about a block up from where she left camera range. I caught up with the bus driver who has that route, and she thinks that a woman who looks like Michelle might have boarded her bus around 11:30 and exited at the train station. I haven't been able to find anyone who saw her after that, but I'm going to try to get access to the station's security tapes."

"Probably not going to happen without a court order," I said. "If it comes to that, I have a friend who's a judge."

"Let's keep that in our back pocket," Collins said. "I have less formal ways that may work. But it may take awhile."

"What was the woman on the tape wearing? Could you tell if she was in a uniform?"

"Didn't seem to be a uniform. She was in jeans and a plain shirt. No logos that I saw. I'll report back as soon as I learn anything more."

We thanked Collins for the update and hung up. Alicia asked, "Do you think Michelle's headed for another state again?"

"Don't know how she'd afford that. She hasn't worked at Premier Cleaning Services long enough to get a paycheck." I tried to think what I would do if I were broke and scared or guilty or just motivated to get out of Dodge. The possibilities I came up with made me realize I wouldn't survive long without a roof over my head and a bank account to draw on.

Alicia said, "The police reports didn't mention if a robbery happened in addition to the murder and vandalism."

I laid my hand on her shoulder. "Let's not borrow trouble. There seems to be enough coming our way without looking for more."

"Trouble or not, I have five realtor open houses I'm supposed to attend. I guess I could ask one of my agents to cover them."

"Why don't you go? If there's word from anyone, I'll give you a call."

After much internal debate, Alicia decided to go to work. I figured I needed to do the same, only my work was tracking down my errant sister-in-law.

I was still special counsel for Klein, Matthews, and

Keller, the law firm I co-founded in Los Angeles. My early retirement from the firm didn't cut me off from the resources available to a practicing attorney. Occasionally, I handled some matters for old clients. Most of the time, though, I merely phoned in to say hello to my paralegal, Lily, or some of the partners. But that morning I called in some favors. I gave Lily a long list of items to check out. If Premier Cleaning Services, Highland Medical, or the late researcher, Dr. Sloan, had any legal actions taken against them, I'd soon know.

Then I called in my big gun. Santa Barbara Superior Court Judge Quentin Jefferson was a law school chum of mine as well as my golfing buddy. I knew if anyone could pick up the inside scoop on what the police were investigating, it was Quentin.

"Finally break free enough for a round of golf Saturday?" Quentin's clear baritone made him a favorite in his church choir. "Between the City Council, your family, and your massage business, it seems like you don't have time anymore for your poor suffering friends who long to get some fresh air and sunshine."

I ignored the rather pathetic tone in his voice and said, "Can I get back to you on that? Right now, I've got a few problems." I filled him in on Michelle and her possible involvement in the Highland Medical melee. "Do you think you can check with your friends in blue and see if Michelle is still on their radar?"

"If she was, don't you think they'd have a posse out after her?"

"Good point. They asked us about her, but I don't know if they checked with anyone else. I guess I want to know how interested they are in finding her." I considered whether having the police search for my sister-in-law was a good thing or a bad thing. I didn't come to a conclusion. "If you find out they are looking for her, then we'll know they think she was involved in some way. Like as a witness." I hurriedly added that last, lest the worst of my fears be verbalized. "If they're not, then I guess we're dealing with Michelle deciding to run away again and we'll have to wait for the private investigator to do her magic."

"You'd think you'd have your hands full with the city's problems. Doesn't seem fair you've got Michelle adding to the mess."

"The world does whirl whether we like it or not. But I've got one really nice thing happening. Ben wants me to adopt him."

"I've always liked that boy. If you turn him down, tell him I'm available. Maybe I'd get to see you more if we were related. Want to adopt me while you're at it?"

Before hanging up, I promised to give Quentin a call later if I found I could squeeze in a round of golf some morning. I checked off the phone calls from my mental list of things to do today and considered the rest of the steps I'd concocted at my 2:00 a.m. planning session that took the place of sleep.

Dr. Kyle Hench, the charming spokesperson for Highland Medical, appeared next on my list. I called, using my position on the council to pry open a meeting time with the gentleman later that day. I felt somewhat guilty since my goal involved gathering information on the cleaning crew and the murder, neither of which concerned the City Council. Then I realized I could throw in Red's Montecito Energized Against Pollution concerns about the disposal of toxic chemicals.

With time before my appointment, I wrote up my suggestions for nonlethal methods for dealing with the ground squirrel problem based on my conversation with Sophia Carlotti. I emailed Sanchez and asked for his opinion on the issue. I didn't share my actual draft, since that would be a violation of California's Brown Act that tries to ensure transparency in government, but I wanted someone else's ideas before I finished crafting my proposal.

A text from Collins came in as I was sending off the last email. "No sign M left SB on bus or train. Will check other transportation hubs."

I concluded that Michelle didn't have the money for a run out of town. She must have returned to the shelter to pick up her things, otherwise she would have no physical resources whatsoever. With only the shirt on her back, it was unlikely she could remain undetected.

My phone's timer beeped to remind me I needed to leave for my appointment with Dr. Hench. I took my notebook and jumped in the car.

****

The Highland Medical Research facility sat on about an acre of land on the outskirts of the city. The building itself proclaimed to the world that this was a state-of-the-art facility. Clean lines and stainless-steel accents complemented the blue-tinted windows and glass doors. The structure was four stories tall and long and wide enough that I imagined three holes of a golf course could fit inside.

The lobby area was equally sleek. Glass-topped coffee tables and plush, leather couches lined two walls. The reception desk commanded the scene. Its black, shiny surface dimly reflected the contents of the room. The young man at the desk welcomed me, and I stated my business. I never got to find out if those couches were as comfortable as they looked since a woman appeared from the back and escorted me to Dr. Hench's office almost before I got my name out.

Dr. Kyle Hench wore his television smile when he greeted me. It was a better look on him than the scowl he'd exhibited at the animal shelter. We shook hands, and I sat in a chair made of material that looked like the reception area couches. It was heavenly.

"I wonder if I could ask you a few things about Highland Medical and your operations."

He spread his hands wide. "As long as it's not proprietary information or a peek into our pharmaceutical labs, I'm always glad to share with the City Council."

My legal career included years of experience judging witnesses and gauging how they parsed their words. Hench, I figured, had an equal amount of practice as a spokesperson for the company and nothing damaging would escape his lips. "I appreciate your candor," I said, returning his glib smile with one of my own. "Maybe we should start with your role in the company."

"You could say I'm a little of everything. Right now, we're a small company, so I'm the chief operating officer in charge of research and development, but I also do research. I handle the press. And I oversee personnel."

"All of that can't leave you with much time for research."

"True, but all new treatment ideas are discussed with me before they're put into development. My scientists devise the treatments and run the first-round tests in the lab, but I supervise them and give direction. I do most of the beta drug trials and submit those results to the government to obtain permission for trials with humans."

"Do you carry out drug trials with people here?"

"Oh, no. Those are done in clinical sites under the supervision of medical doctors. My job is to apply for permits from the Federal Drug Administration for any new drugs we develop and to detail the protocol we use with animals. People don't realize the amount of work that goes into finding new treatments. From the point that we develop a possible new drug to the time when consumers can buy it is about twelve years."

"That's a long time."

"Actually, that's on the short end. It can take three-and-a-half years in lab time to produce a new drug. And then, only about five in every five thousand drugs that enter preclinical testing make it to human trials. Of the five that go through the human trial phase, only one is approved by the FDA to be sold. In fact, only about twenty-three NMEs are approved each year."

"NMEs?"

"Sorry. I slip into vernacular sometimes. NMEs are New Molecular Entities. A fancy name for new drugs."

"That seems like a lot of effort for very little result."

"That's why we have so many drugs in development at the same time. Obviously, the more lab space we have, the more tests we can run and the more cures we can deliver."

"Potential cures."

Hench raised both his eyebrows and said, "You sound like our lawyers."

"I've been told that before. Tell me how the rewards work on something like a new drug. I mean, when a baseball team wins a World Series, the players aren't the only ones rewarded. Everyone in the organization gets a diamond-encrusted ring. Does it work like that in a lab?"

"That depends on the company. Highland Medical does believe in incentivizing research, and it's safe to say that successes are rewarded. There are bonuses when we have a drug go to trial and a bigger bonus if it's approved as an NME. The bonuses are shared because many times our research builds off each other's work." He coughed. "Of course, the exact details of the bonuses and their distribution are proprietary information."

"Of course." I decided to head off any further lectures and return to the reason I came. "What are your duties with personnel?"

"I recruit and hire the researchers. I also determine how many research assistants we need to hire, and I do an orientation session with those. In fact, we just got a new batch in and I'm very pleased with how well they're working out."

I debated mentioning Ben but decided a low profile might be a better choice. "And do your duties also involve supervision of the test animals or the disposal of any toxic chemicals used in the facility?"

"I approve the purchase of test subjects, but the ordering and care of them fell to Dr. Sloan. Since his unfortunate death, I've taken over that role temporarily." He leaned forward and regarded me more closely. "Weren't you at the Humane Society yesterday?"

"Yes. Sean called me because he wasn't sure what to do. I told him to notify Highland."

"You did the right thing. It's dangerous for those animals to be out of the lab. Most need to be kept on closely monitored medications, and the animal shelter people couldn't handle that."

"So, they've been returned?"

"Our lawyers are working on it. In the meantime, the shelter has allowed some of our people to bring medication to the animals and monitor their condition."

"Were those the only animals Highland has?"

"Not at all. That group was involved with only one disease. We have different kennels for each of the projects we have going."

"And the chemical disposal?"

"Is there some problem with that?"

"Some members of the public have expressed their concerns."

"That's quite common with the general public. They don't really understand the way things work." Hench went on to explain how the company ensured that all chemical and waste products were packaged and quarantined until the hazardous waste disposal company picked them up.

"Do you train your cleaning crew in these methods as well?"

"We have an outside company do the general cleaning. None of that is inside areas where any potentially harmful materials are found. The labs and kennels are cleaned by the research assistants who are trained in all the safety measures."

"Then the cleaners from the outside company never get near the lab or kennel areas?"

"Only the hallways outside those areas. All the sensitive areas are kept locked. They are only accessible through a keypad, and that combination changes frequently."

A small measure of relief washed over me. Michelle could not have gotten into the lab where the scientist was killed. Her disappearance must be due to other factors.

Hench frowned. "Is this about our expansion plans? I can assure you that the same safety protocols will be in place in the new wing as well."

I put on my best courtroom face. "That was one reason. I wonder if I could have a tour of your facility—the public areas—as well as study your plans." Whatever the hell those may be, I added to myself. No expansion plans had appeared before the council or the planning department that I was aware of.

"We don't usually give tours of our facility. Security reasons, you know." Hench tapped his fingertips on the desk. "But for the City Council, anything."

The tour was impressive and uninformative. Besides seeing four stories of gleaming hallways, well-furnished offices, and locked doors, I learned nothing germane to my quest.

Hench led the way through a hallway of the research portion of the center that was located on the ground floor of the facility. I saw crime scene tape sealing off the entry to a door at the far end of the hall. He stopped in the middle of the hall to describe the labs behind the locked doors and some of the diseases they were trying to treat.

I noticed a door that was partially ajar on the opposite side of the hall. "What's this?" I asked and pulled the door open. I saw brooms and mops as well as boxes stacked on shelves. Although a cleaning cart took up much of the interior, enough room remained for a person to step into the space and root through all the materials. A uniform shirt with a Premier Cleaning Services logo lay draped across the top shelf of the cart.

"It's a utility closet. It has emergency supplies in it, so it's kept unlocked. The door is supposed to be closed, however." He looked inside. "What's this cart doing here? One more thing to talk to our cleaning company about." He shut the door.

A lab door opened in the hallway ahead of us. A woman stepped out who I thought fit the stereotype of a female scientist with precision. Her greying blonde hair was caught up in a bun on the back of her head. She was thin and wore a white lab coat and black-rimmed glasses. Behind those glasses, her eyes were swollen and red-rimmed. I wondered how close she'd been to Dr. Sloan.

Hench paused to introduce us. "This is Dr. Ingrid Olsson. She was Dr. Sloan's associate and is now in charge of his projects as well as her own."

I shook hands with Dr. Olsson, noting the blue eyes that completed the Swedish package. Her face was vaguely familiar. "Have we met before?"

Her eyes swept my face before she replied, "No."

"I'm sorry for your loss."

She glanced at me sharply, as if confused, then said, "Oh. Dr. Sloan. Yes."

"You're in charge of Dr. Sloan's test subjects now?"

She flicked a glance at Hench. "Yes. And if the Humane Society would only return the animals they have, it would make my life a lot easier. I need to compare their progress with our alpha test subjects."

No personable smile accompanied the request, only a petulant scowl. I wondered if the company appointed Dr. Hench spokesperson because he was the only one who could at least pretend to be human.

Dr. Olsson turned to Hench. "I really do need to speak with you soon regarding the experiments. There are a few things that don't make sense."

After Hench promised to stop by later that afternoon, I addressed Dr. Olsson, "What did you think of Dr. Sloan and his work?"

"Nathan was a dedicated researcher. A man of great integrity. He also possessed a brilliant mind. I'm sure his latest theory on an immunotherapy drug to cure a type of childhood lymphoma will be a success." Olsson took a deep breath, as if stringing together that many words drained her. "He'll be missed."

That seemed like a flat ending to a tribute, but since Sloan wasn't my main interest, I switched to something closer to home. "Is it possible to see your lab?"

Olsson started to refuse, but then said, "All right. There's one where no one's working right now, so you won't be disturbing anything. But don't touch the animals or any equipment." She blocked my view as she punched in numbers on the keypad located on the wall beside the door.

"Is that a personal code or is it one everyone uses?"

Hench answered. "Each section of the building has its own entry code that is changed on an irregular basis. Since each section is working on a cure for the same or related diseases, we sometimes need to access each other's labs to check records and compare notes."

Workers not having an individual code would mean there would be no way of knowing who opened any particular door and when. Seemed like a shoddy security system to me. I looked up and down the shiny hallway and across the ceiling. "I see you do have security cameras in place. Didn't they help you identify the person who broke in?"

"The lenses were blurred. It appears the cleaning crew was overzealous a few days ago and tried to wipe them off. The police suggested that we install cages around the cameras. That way nobody could reach them to tamper with them."

"Wouldn't your security team have noticed the blurred lenses?"

"The hallway cameras aren't monitored. They're motion sensitive and only record when activated."

Olsson swung the door open and gestured us through. The sterile-looking room featured a concrete floor. Shelves and cages lined two walls of the room. Six layers of shelving spaced about a foot apart stood on one-half of the left-hand wall. Those shelves held glass cages with wire mesh tops and sawdust-lined bottoms. The rest of the shelves were farther apart, allowing for the larger cages that filled them. Twelve of the cages appeared large enough to hold a primate. A four-inch by six-inch rectangular frame attached to the front of each cage looked like a plastic-name-badge holder.

The cages I saw held mice, guinea pigs, and rabbits. The animals looked a lot healthier than the ones taken in by the Humane Society. Although patches of fur were shaved off the various body parts of some animals, on the whole they looked perky and well-fed. Only a few were listless enough to ignore us when we went by their cages.

"These animals appear to be in good shape. Aren't you using them to test cures?"

Olsson sounded offended as she replied, "Dr. Sloan took excellent care of his animals. All of these subjects have a form of B-cell lymphoma and are being used to find a cure for that. It was a passion of Nathan's."

I blinked. "Wait. This is Dr. Sloan's lab? I thought he was killed in his lab."

Hench answered. "No. He was in my lab. The one at the end of the hall."

"What was he doing in your lab?"

"I wish I knew." Hench sounded irritated. "It was highly unusual. Not only that, he had no reason to be in the building in the evening. We encourage all of our researchers to keep regular hours. He never mentioned any special project that would necessitate him checking on his experiments at night." He turned to Olsson. "Did he say anything to you?"

She shook her head. "We weren't at any critical point with any of the tests. We should have some new data in the next three weeks. The trial of the derivative of methotrexate is showing promise. So is the immunotherapy treatment."

As the two scientists discussed the drug trial, I continued my stroll around the lab. An eight-foot-long, stainless-steel table occupied the center of the room, like an island in a kitchen. Smaller rolling carts with racks, test tubes, and boxes of syringes rested next to it. A refrigeration chamber occupied part of the back wall. On the other side of the wall, two three-drawer file cabinets stood. In between the files and the fridge was an eight-foot sliding door that faced the outside wall. Two bolted locks, each with padlocks shut tight, secured the door.

I pointed to the sliding door. "Where does that lead?"

Olsson looked up. "That's a loading dock. Some of the animals and equipment require a large opening to enter the building. The first five rooms on this side of the building open onto the dock. Four are labs and one is a storage area for new animals and equipment."

"Could someone enter from any of those?"

"Highly unlikely." Hench pulled out his keychain and dangled a key. "The locks can only be opened from the inside, and only three of us have keys to the loading dock doors: the plant manager, the head of security, and me."

I tried to think of a question that would give me more insight into Michelle's disappearance. I failed. I decided to keep up appearances instead. "Will the animal areas in the new wing be like this?"

Hench's professional smile reappeared. Without saying a word to Olsson, he waved me out the door of the lab and into the hallway. "Let me show you."

Chapter Eleven

When I arrived home from my tour of Highland Medical, Alicia was in the bedroom changing from her office clothes into jeans, a cotton blouse, and hiking boots.

While she changed, I told her about my visit to Highland Medical. I concluded, "There's no way Michelle could have had anything to do with the whole fiasco at the lab. The actual labs don't get cleaned by her company, and the lab where the killing took place was locked. No way for her to get in there. So, we need to wait for Keesha to track her down. And Quentin got back to me. According to him, the police aren't putting a great deal of effort into finding Michelle. They're looking into a more private motive. It seems like he wanted to say something else, but he wouldn't cough up more than that."

"Quentin is always the model of discretion. Maybe you can find out more if you set up a golf game with him. You said he's been bugging you about that."

"With all that's going on, I don't think wandering around a golf course is the best use of my time. But you may be right that Quentin would tell me something in person that he wouldn't say over the phone."

"Whatever excuse you need to deceive yourself so that you can play golf, go for it." She finished tying the last bow on her boot. "I'm going to check out a lead one of the realtors gave me. Evidently, there's an encampment near Rattlesnake Canyon."

"Rattlesnake Canyon?" The hazy image of a stone bridge and a lot of manzanita floated in my brain. We hiked there in the first blush of excitement when we moved to Santa Barbara. But I'd heard or seen that name recently. But where? Dormant brain synapses kicked in gear. "I told you Hench showed me the layout for Highland Medical's expansion. Along with the architectural drawings he showed me a map of the overall area. Rattlesnake Canyon isn't far from the building."

I could almost see Alicia flipping through her mental map of the city. How someone so competent with directions could be attracted to someone like me who could get lost on her way to the living room is one of the great mysteries of love.

"You're right. It's fairly close to it. Less than two miles west if you could go straight across, which you can't. Unless there are some woodland trails." Alicia sat up straighter. "If Michelle knew about that camp, and she disappeared from the lab, she might have headed there."

"Give me a chance to change, and I'll go with you."

"Bring cash," Alicia called to me. "We might need to provide incentive."

****

We reached Skofield Park, the gateway to Rattlesnake Canyon, in twenty minutes. The sandstone bridge I remembered still existed. It marked the trailhead through the canyon. A five-minute trek brought us to a gravel track that quickly became a dusty, dirt path that paralleled a meandering stream that flowed fifteen feet below. Purple sage, manzanita, and abundant red-fruited toyon bushes lined the path.

As we rounded one of the serpentine curves that gave the trail its name, I saw a woman ahead of us carrying a reusable canvas grocery bag. She wore blue scrubs such as a nurse might wear. Not exactly normal hiking clothes. I tapped Alicia's arm and signaled her to drop back behind the protruding branches of a bush.

The woman glanced over her shoulder before turning and whistling a sharp note. She lifted one of the branches of a sage bush and stepped off the trail.

We hurried to the spot where the woman disappeared. A casual hiker would have overlooked the slight break in between the otherwise dense growth of bushes and trees. I quietly slid into the gap with Alicia following. I pushed through some branches that blocked my way before coming to a clearing that was flat and open like a meadow.

I expected a rag-tag collection of tents and lean-tos fashioned from cardboard. There were, indeed, about a dozen weathered nylon tents. But there were also four, make-shift, canvas structures that might shelter up to six people each. Three fire rings surrounded by stones stood in the open area in front of the shelters. They were spaced about ten feet apart. Several people sat or squatted beside fires in two of the pits. The quiet burbling of the stream could be heard coming from the far side of the encampment.

Our crunching through the bushes must have alerted them because most turned to stare at us.

One man unfolded himself from his position by the fire. His shaved head and snake tattoos across his upper arms and exposed chest gave him a less than friendly air. That impression was reinforced when he clasped a stout stick and advanced toward us.

I raised my open hands up in the air. "We're not here to make trouble. We're trying to find our sister."

"Back down, Leo." The woman in the hospital uniform touched the bare bicep of the tattooed man. She placed the canvas shopping bag on the ground, crossed her arms, and glared at us. "You should leave now."

Although it was undoubtedly sage advice, I stepped forward. "Please. Just listen to us, and if you can't help us, we'll go away."

By now the rest of the camp was standing in a semicircle around the nurse and snake man. Most were women of varying ages, although there were a few older males. Alicia slid to my side. She addressed the growing crowd. "My sister is ill and needs medication. She left her work Tuesday and hasn't been seen since. She's been homeless before, and we think she may have run off again. We only want to talk with her and make sure she's all right. Please."

No one spoke, so I slid the photo of Michelle out of my pocket and hesitantly crept toward the nurse. I presumed she was their leader, if camps such as these observed any organizational structure. I held out the photo and said, "Her name is Michelle, but she also goes by Shelly."

No one took the photo, but I swept the picture around the group at eye level.

Again, it was the nurse who spoke. "Are you police or something?"

"No, ma'am. We're her family."

She snorted. "Ma'am? Sheesh. I'm probably half your age."

"Mom!" The shout preceded two children galloping across the grassy space that separated the fire pit area from the taller trees on the other side of camp. The two threw themselves on the nurse, and she gave them each a quick kiss on their heads.

She handed the older one the cloth bag she'd placed on the ground. "Take this to Beverly, honey. Be careful. There are eggs today." The boy and girl, who I judged to be about ten and twelve, headed toward one of the tents with their precious cargo.

"Beverly?"

"Yeah. My partner." She looked us up and down. "You got something to say about that?"

"No." I clipped the "ma'am" off before it slipped out of my mouth. Instead, I explained to the ensemble about Michelle and our search for her. "She was last seen about a mile from here, so we were wondering if she came by."

A teenager wearing torn jeans and a work shirt said, "A lot of people on the road don't exactly want to be found, if you know what I mean. What if this sister of yours is one of them?"

Alicia said, "I don't think she wants to disappear. She been on medication, and it really seems to have helped her. She has a job and everything."

The nurse laughed. "Half the people here are on meds of one kind or another. And a lot of us have jobs. We're still here."

"Why is that?" I asked. At her skeptical stare, I said, "I really want to know why you choose to be out here instead of in an apartment or public housing."

The woman erupted. "Choose? *Choose?* Do you have any idea how much an apartment costs? First month rent plus security. Then there are the utilities. If you don't have credit, you need to make a down payment for gas and water and electricity if the apartment doesn't cover that. Beverly and I have saved up for five months, ever since I got this job as a nursing assistant at the hospital. Bev has two jobs cleaning and waitressing. And we're still not close to what we need. It's not like we're sitting around the campfire waiting for a handout."

The teen interrupted. "What if we are choosing to be here? What if we don't want to be part of the patriarchal, rat-race, pharmacy-run, screwed-up world out there? What if we don't want the government reading our thoughts through all the electronics they've got planted all over the country?" She narrowed her eyes at me. "Hey, maybe you're one of those government Nazis."

The growl of discontent that followed this pronounce-ment made me glad I hadn't mentioned my City Council sta-tus. "Look, we only want to know if Michelle came through here. If you have any information about her, there's a reward."

The nurse pointed behind us. "I'd get out now while you can."

Alicia and I made as graceful an exit through the bushes as possible while not turning our backs to the crowd. Once safely on the trail, we picked leaves out of each other's hair.

Alicia sighed. "When Michelle first ran away, she said the same thing that girl did about people spying on her. That she needed to get away, to hide. If someone's sure everyone is out to get them, how do you convince them that you're the exception? That you really want to help?"

I shrugged, having nothing to offer in the way of expla-nation.

A rustling in the trees made us jump.

The daughter of the nursing assistant appeared in the pathway. "You said there's a reward. How much money are you talking about?"

"Did you see Michelle?" I asked, holding out the photo to her.

She nodded.

"When?"

"Tuesday night. It was after dark. She came into our camp. Mom wasn't there, but Beverly said we should feed her and put her up for a night. But then a tree branch broke with a big crack. That woman jumped up and pulled a gun out of the bag she carried. When Beverly saw that, she told your sister she needed to leave. We don't allow guns in our home."

"Do you know where she went?"

The girl crossed her arms in much the same way her mother had. "What about that reward?"

Glad of Alicia's forewarning of the need for cash, I pulled two twenties out of my pocket. At her haughty look of disdain, I pulled out two more.

She folded the money and slid it into her front pocket then pointed down the road to the beginning of the path. "Beverly told her how to get to Skofield Park and where to get the bus from there."

"Did Beverly tell her where another camp might be that she could go to?"

"Yeah. She said it was too late to get a bed at any of the shelters, so she should talk to Lefty at Gutierrez Park. The buses run near there."

Damn, I thought. So, nice, ex-Marine Lefty lied to me. Another trip to the warehouses of Gutierrez Street loomed in the near future.

* * * *

I stared out our picture windows at the ever-churning ocean. Clouds obscured our view of the Channel Islands, an apt metaphor for the fog my mind seemed to be experiencing.

When I proposed driving straight over to Lefty's campsite, Alicia nixed the idea. She reasoned that if he didn't tell us anything this morning, it wasn't likely he'd changed his mind in a few hours.

We spent the trip home mulling over Michelle's peculiarities and how they might factor into her disappearance. The discussion continued at home.

Alicia paced the living room. "Okay, let's be logical. Michelle's probably off her meds and she's scared. No cash, no credit card. She may not be thinking clearly enough to figure out a way out of town. Keesha hasn't found a trace of her at the shelters or on the streets, so she must be hiding somewhere else that doesn't require any form of payment."

"Another homeless encampment?"

"Maybe, but I've got another idea. I need my computer."

In under an hour, my wife consulted her realtor website and compiled a list of all the vacant houses in the Central Coast region, highlighted the ones in the sections of towns that might be more susceptible to squatters, and was out the door. She refused my counsel of caution and my offers of help. Short of trailing after her in my car, the best I could do was obtain a copy of her research and elicit promises to be home by dark and to call every half hour as a safety check.

With Alicia on a mission, I was left in a house that was empty aside from a cat who demanded an early dinner. I fed Ginger, called Collins to inform her of Alicia's quest, and felt myself slump into a torpor of gloom.

Ginger thanked me for the meal by rubbing against my leg. I picked her up, carried her into the office, and placed her beside my computer. She curled into a contented, purring ball as I scrolled through my emails. I clicked on one from my law office.

My crack paralegal, Lily, came through yet again. Not only did she search legal files but also news reports. Her preliminary report gave me much to consider.

Highland Medical's ancestry was hazy. Its parent corporation seemed to be a part of a conglomerate with two other companies, neither of which was in the medical field. She noted that she was still working on the company's lineage and its current owners and major shareholders. She found Highland filed two Investigational New Drug applications (or IND, she noted) with the Federal Drug Administration since opening in Santa Barbara. She helpfully included the explanation that a drug company must submit an IND to the FDA for approval on a new drug before it could be used in clinical trials in humans. One of Highland's drugs had entered Phase I of clinical trials. The other was pending approval.

Lily could find no police record for the late Dr. Nathan Sloan. He was divorced, with two children. Wife was awarded full custody. Four months ago, his ex-wife filed with the court for relief because Sloan was six months behind on his child support payments. No action was taken since Sloan fulfilled his overdue obligation two months ago.

Lily's report went on to say that Sloan's will was filed for probate. His children were beneficiaries of his life insurance and fifty percent of his net worth. He left the rest of his estate to a variety of charities including one for cancer research. As I glanced down the list of organizations, I spotted a familiar name: Animals First.

I reached out and scratched Ginger's chin as I pondered. A guy who experiments on animals left some of his estate to an animal rights organization?

I stared out my study window at the grey, undulating waves of the ocean. Each hill of water rolling in was a separate entity, but once it crashed on the sand, it was swept back into the ocean to become part of the next wave. This mixing and mingling of murky water mirrored the myriad facts and suppositions swirling in my mind.

Would any of this put me any closer to finding Michelle?

As if the thought of Michelle activated universal forces, my phone rang with Alicia's half-hour check in.

"No progress on Michelle," Alicia said. "But I saw an old apartment building on the border of Santa Barbara and Goleta that might be great for housing homeless. They're already squatting there, and it's been on the market for almost a year. It would be nice if the city bought it and turned on the electricity and running water."

"The dear mayor has already spewed forth a few choice words at me about my spendthrift ways. But I might throw that into the mix of my proposal."

Alicia blew electronic kisses before signing off. I could tell this quest, whether it be a Don Quixote venture or not, was good for her. Her voice sounded stronger and more positive.

The phone rang again, this time with Sarah on the other end of the line.

"The police arrested Sophia Carlotti for the murder of that Highland Medical doctor, Sloan."

Chapter Twelve

Sophia Carlotti slumped at my kitchen table, hands wrapped tightly around a mug of hot, black coffee. "Some big shit like Sloan gets blown away, and the police are all over it, picking up anyone who's the least bit connected with him. But a poor kid like Jeff? He's been dead a week and do you hear anything about him? Hell no."

As soon as I heard about Carlotti being brought in for Sloan's murder, I called a criminal defense lawyer I knew and used more times than I liked. She agreed to go to the police station to see if Carlotti wanted to use her services. To the surprise of both of us, Carlotti agreed.

I wasn't amazed to learn that the internet news my daughter relied on was wrong. The police did not officially arrest Carlotti but merely brought her in for questioning, so our lawyer was able to get her released. I asked her to bring the intrepid animal rights activist to our house, and again to my wonder, Carlotti agreed. The lawyer left soon after depositing her in our kitchen. It was my guess that she didn't want to be around in case Carlotti said anything incriminating.

"Did you tell the police anything?" I asked.

She glared at the mug as if it were the one who dragged her to the police station. "No. I told them as little as possible. On the advice of your friend. There's not much to tell, anyway. I was at the loading dock. I heard howling. The door to the lab was cracked open, so I decided to check things out." She shook her head. "There were dozens of animals jumping around in their cages, shrieking. Howling. It was horrible. Electrodes poking out of their skulls. Tumors under their skin. All of them scared and screaming. I knew I had to rescue them."

"The door wasn't locked?"

"No. I told you. It was slightly open. I think that's why I was able to hear the animals."

"What about Dr. Sloan?"

"You mean the guy on the floor? Yeah, he was obviously dead. Gunshot wound to the chest. Way too much blood loss. I did check his neck to make sure. He was gone."

I puzzled over the fact that Carlotti didn't react to Sloan's name despite her organization being named in his will. I let it slide for the moment. "Did you hear a gunshot before you opened the door?"

She shook her head. "Just the animals. Must have missed the kill by a few minutes. That guy was warm, and his blood was still fresh, but no more was pumping out of him. Might have hit the heart directly or maybe blasted open the aorta. He must have bled out fast."

Carlotti spoke like one who had experienced violent death too many times. She reported the specifics of Sloan's death without emotion. The details were more than I wanted to hear, but I probed anyway. "Were there any footsteps in the blood or any indication that someone else was in the room with him?"

"You trying to make this out to be a suicide?" Carlotti shook her head again. "No bloody footprints, and no gun anywhere around. The guy must have been packing, though. He wore an empty shoulder holster."

"Shoulder holster? Like a concealed gun?"

"Yep." She didn't sound impressed or surprised.

"Did you check out the hallway?" I asked, getting to the crux of why I wanted to talk with Carlotti.

Carlotti stared at me as if I'd asked if little green men were wandering through the lab. "There's a dead guy in a pool of blood, and I'm somewhere I'm not supposed to be, and you're asking me if I took time to crack open the door and get seen by somebody, or worse yet, find Rambo outside with his gun ready for round two? You must think I'm a friggin' idiot."

I'd hoped she could shed light on Michelle's whereabouts at the time of the murder, but I believed her caution in not wanting to go near the doorway. I let her get some sips of coffee in her before asking, "So why, exactly, did you happen to be on the loading dock of Sloan's lab at Highland Medical?"

Shutters slid down behind Carlotti's eyes. "Like I told the cops, I was driving by and I stopped when a big rig backed out of the parking lot and took up the whole street. Before it took off down the street, I spotted a cat on the loading dock. I went up there to rescue it."

"Did you mention to them about going into the lab?"

"What lab? All I did was pick up the cat and put it into one of the crates I always carry in my truck."

It took a moment for me to realize that she was cutting me off. "So, the police don't know you were in there, and you didn't admit to rescuing the animals inside the lab."

Carlotti merely blew across the top of the coffee.

"And I presume this conversation never happened."

Carlotti gulped down the remainder of the coffee, swung her artificial leg to the side of the chair, and hoisted herself up. "Thanks for the lawyer. Not that I'll need one. My prints are nowhere in that lab, and there were no security cameras operating inside the lab. All the police have is that my truck was seen on the surveillance camera entering the parking lot of the lab. If anyone says anything different, I'll deny it. Clear?"

I stood. "Thank you for telling me the whole story."

Carlotti shrugged on her jacket. "Nobody ever tells the whole story. Especially if money or the government are involved. And Highland is covered in both piles of shit."

****

"I understand you bailed Sophia Carlotti out of jail. Are you providing counsel for her as well?" John Johnson phoned this time rather than trying for an in-person interview.

Given his incorrect assessment of the situation, I knew he was fishing. I also knew better than to give him ammunition. "I have no comment."

"Are you in league with Carlotti? She's filed several lawsuits against Highland Medical for their treatment of animals. All of them were thrown out of court for lack of evidence. Are you supporting her cause?"

"No comment."

"Maybe you'd like to say something about your

sister-in-law and son both working at Highland Medical. Are they collecting information for you and Carlotti? Or is their employment payback for you from Highland for supporting their city subsidies?"

"No comment."

"Jeffrey Henderson was investigating Highland Medical, and he was close to breaking open a major scandal. Now he's dead and a scientist at Highland is dead. I don't think it's a coincidence, do you?" At my silence, Johnson sighed. "Look, I moved to Santa Barbara six months ago, and I already see how much corruption there is in the political system. It makes my hometown seem like Disneyland. I'm trying to uncover the rot. If you're part of it, I'll bring you down. If you're not, then help me out here. It seems like there's a coverup going on."

"Mr. Johnson, I'm sure you're trying to do your best as a reporter. But remember, reporters are supposed to report the news, not make it up. Get your facts straight, and then, maybe, we can talk."

****

"Wine. Then maybe food." Alicia dropped her purse on the kitchen counter. "I had no idea how many people live on the streets. We have to do something about this."

I uncorked a Cabernet and poured Alicia a glass.

She took it into the living room and collapsed onto the couch. She held the glass without drinking. "I sometimes forget how good we have it. This incredible home. Our kids. Our friends. Even simple things, like running water, heat, electricity. We are so blessed."

I sat beside her and slid an arm around her shoulders. "We are."

Alicia snuggled her head into my shoulder. "I think I handed out more business cards today than I have in the whole of this last year. Next time, I'm going to make care packages to give out as well."

"Does that mean you didn't get through your whole list?"

Alicia shook her head. "Maybe half." She took a belated sip of wine. "What about you? Any word from Keesha?"

"Nothing from our intrepid detective, but I picked up some interesting tidbits, nonetheless." I told her of Lily's research into the life of Dr. Sloan and of my visit with the police "person of interest" Sophia Carlotti. "Sophia left me with the impression that she knew a lot more about Highland Medical than she was willing to share."

"Do you believe she didn't kill him?"

I shrugged. "What do I know about killers? That's why I went into corporate law. More money, less bullets. I merely wanted to find out if she saw Michelle."

Alicia ignored my non-answer. "I wonder why the cargo door was open."

"Maybe the killer left that way, in a hurry."

She hummed a low tone, which I knew meant she was processing information. "I guess that makes more sense than going out through the hallways. Why risk being seen by anyone who might have heard the shot?" Her eyes widened. "If that's the case, wouldn't Sophia have seen the killer, or, at least, a car driving away?"

"Great question. One I should have thought of."

"You can't always think of everything, dear," Alicia said, and patted my hand. "That's why you have me." She grew serious. "Sophia probably feels a great deal of sympathy for someone who gets rid of a doctor who tortures animals. Maybe enough sympathy to cover for the killer?"

****

Dinner consisted of equal parts of eating and planning. Alicia wanted to accompany me the next day to talk with Lefty. Since she was obligated to an early morning real estate appointment, that visit with Lefty would need to be later in the day. With some hours now free, I called Quentin. The honorable judge said he'd be pleased to haul his body out of bed at six in the morning merely for the pleasure of beating me at golf.

Quentin had already hit through most of a bucket of balls by the time I joined him Friday morning at the driving range. An early tee time never deterred Quentin from spending half an hour warming up with at least one large bucket of balls.

I teed up a ball from the small basket that I'd purchased. "It doesn't matter how many practice swings you get in, your golf game still stinks."

"Ah, you don't know how much worse I would be if I didn't limber up beforehand." After another dozen shots, he drove a sizzler straight down the middle of the range. His teeth shone bright in contrast with his dark skin as he turned to me with a smirk. "I think I'll double our usual wager today."

I admired the distance and roll of his shot. "Maybe we should skip the game and go straight to me buying you breakfast."

"No way. I have no intention of missing one minute of your agony as I beat you on every hole. Besides, I have news, but you never heard it from me."

As we headed toward the first hole, Quentin filled me in.

"Something's going on in this case that's piqued the interest of the Feds. And it's ticking off our local boys in blue."

We reached the first hole only to have to wait for the foursome ahead of us to tee off.

I lowered my voice and asked Quentin, "The FBI? Is Highland Medical under investigation?"

Quentin whispered back, "Don't know. Police detectives bring their evidence to the D.A., not a judge, so I'm not in the loop. And no one has asked for any warrants yet, so I don't know where the investigation is headed. Not that I could tell you if I did."

The group ahead of us trudged down the fairway in search of their balls. While Quentin teed up, I thought of what little I knew of the research facility. Could the business be a cover for drug smuggling or money laundering? Seemed like an elaborate scam for a mob to set up.

Quentin took a few practice swings then stepped to the tee. I watched his drive hook into the tree line.

I patted his back as I stepped to the tee. "The tide has turned. Looks like you'll be paying for breakfast after all."

****

A phone call interrupted my drive home. John Johnson, Jr.'s, voice leapt out of the car's speaker. "Got some intel I thought you'd like to know. It seems that Dr. Sloan, the victim at Highland Medical, was a gambler. A bad one. To make up for his losses, he did business with a couple of loan sharks who didn't care for late payments. The rumor is that the doctor might have engaged in some unethical activities in order to earn some quick extra income."

"Such as?"

"Not clear. There's some noise about money laundering, or possibly dealing with illegally importing endangered animal parts like rhino horns, but nothing definite."

I thought of Quentin's comments about FBI involvement. If true, either of Johnson's scenarios would account for the Fed presence. "And why are you telling me this?"

"Jeffrey Henderson thought something fishy was happening at Highland, and it looks like Sloan was mixed up in shady activities. Now both of them are dead. Also, Highland has dealings with the City Council and is a big monetary supporter of political candidates." The reporter cleared his throat. "Then there's the issue of you, a City Council member, who finds Jeff's body, gets your relatives hired at Highland, and hushes up an eyewitness to the crime before the police can fully question her. I've got to wonder how this is all connected."

"Only in your dreams."

****

I tried to shake off Johnson's innuendos as I drove Alicia to the homeless encampment on Gutierrez Street. I noticed that we passed close to the headquarters for Animals First. I prevailed upon Alicia to let me stop and clear up the question I hadn't asked in my meeting with Sophia Carlotti yesterday regarding her seeing anyone else close to Highland Medical.

The door to the office was locked. A handwritten sign announced that Animals First would be closed until further notice. The sign included a phone number for inquiries, but no one answered when I tried it on my cell. I called Carlotti's attorney, but she gave no comment on her client's whereabouts. Defeated for the moment, I returned to the car.

Since it was almost lunchtime, we stopped at a sandwich shop and picked up a dozen assorted subs for distribution at the abandoned warehouse. I hoped food would ensure a warmer welcome than the one we received from the encampment in Rattlesnake Canyon.

The same half-dozen people occupied the same square of lawn as before, with one exception. Lefty was not among them. We showed Michelle's photo again with no success. We handed out sandwiches and asked for Lefty. Vague responses made it seem as if Lefty was someone we conjured from our imagination.

We split one of the sub sandwiches on the way home, chewing our way through the frustrations of the day.

As we pulled into our driveway, I noticed a car parked along our curb with a license plate holder advertising a car dealership in Orange County. Since our street dead-ends at steps that lead to the beach, many people park there, so I didn't think much about an out-of-town car. Or I didn't until I saw Zacharias Wise standing on our front steps. Alicia's face hardened as she caught sight of her ex-husband."Shit," she muttered. "This is the last thing I need today."

Zach had never come to our Santa Barbara home before. We never invited him to visit given the fact that the one time he came to our third-floor condo in Los Angeles, he pushed me against the balcony railing and threatened to throw me over the side. The fact that I wasn't involved in Alicia's decision to divorce him didn't lessen his anger toward me.

I thought the three of us reached détente at Sarah's wedding last year, but Zach's friendly hello contrasted with wary eyes. Nevertheless, we invited him in.

"What are you doing here, Zach?" Alicia's tone was cool as we seated ourselves in the living room.

Zach's eyes took in the room and the view as well as noting the exits. He appeared to have the PTSD under much better control, but I imagined the horrors that he experienced in the Mideast would never allow him to fully relax.

He glanced at me before turning his attention on Alicia. "Sarah told me about Ben and the adoption. I wanted to talk with you about it."

"What's there to discuss?" Alicia asked.

"I'd think that you'd contact me. Ben's my son."

Alicia leaned forward, hands clasped and bent elbows on her knees. I could tell she was fighting for control of her emotions. "Ben is a grown man. He made this request himself. If he wanted to talk it over with you, I'm sure he would have called you. Since he didn't, I guess he didn't think it was any of your business."

"Of course it's my business. He's turning his back on me, his father. He's acting like I'm dead."

"Face it, Zach. You've never had a relationship with Ben."

"Whose fault is that? You went to court and took away my right to see my kids. You never let Ben get to know me."

Alicia snapped. "Don't give me that crap. You didn't bother using your visitation rights. You didn't like being supervised by a social worker when you were with the kids. The judge told you that you could apply for unsupervised visitation once you completed a year of sobriety. But you didn't bother to do that either. Instead, you went out and got yourself a new wife and a new batch of kids. You were the one to turn your back on Sarah and Ben."

Zach's face turned red. He stood and wheeled toward me, jabbing his finger at my face. "You're trying to steal my son. I won't have it."

"I don't think you have any say in the matter."

"We'll see about that," Zach said, as he slammed the door behind him.

His exit did nothing to erase the angry energy that almost vibrated in our living room. Safety was my first concern. "Does Zach know where Ben lives?"

Alicia shook her head then frowned. "Unless Sarah told him." She grabbed her phone and dialed.

I sat beside Alicia so I could hear the conversation, too. Sarah answered on the third ring. I heard office sounds in the background. In answer to Alicia's question, Sarah said, "I might have mentioned the area Ben lives in, but I never gave Dad the address. Why? What's happened now?"

"Your father was just at the house. He was not in the best of tempers when he left. We're afraid he may confront Ben."

"I can't believe Dad would hurt Ben."

I snorted. "You didn't see him when he charged out of here."

My muttered comment must have made it over the airwaves since Sarah said, "Look, Dad isn't like that. You don't know him like I do."

In all the years we've been together, Alicia never said anything bad about Zach to the kids. She reassured them the divorce had nothing to do with them. She softened the emotional blows when each birthday and Hanukkah passed without word from their father. This time, I thought the dam might break.

I was wrong.

Alicia took a deep breath. "We'll talk later." She pushed the disconnect button and tossed the phone onto the coffee table before slumping against my shoulder. "Someday, I'm going to kill that girl."

"Frankly, I'm surprised it hasn't happened before now." I kissed the top of her head. "Should we call Ben and warn him about Zach?"

Alicia sighed and reached once more for her phone.

Once I heard he hadn't received a visit from his father, I left them to discuss the situation and headed to my office. I wanted to document all the places we'd been to hunt for Michelle and the results of each. While composing that list, my mind drifted to Carlotti and the Highland Medical murder. Why was the animal rights crusader at the loading dock that led to Hench's medical experimentation lab? Why was Sloan there? Was Carlotti meeting Sloan by design? Why did Sloan leave money to Carlotti's organization in his will? How were those two involved? Was there more to their relationship than a concern for animals? Given Sloan's occupation, it seemed illogical that the two were bonding over a mutual concern for animal welfare.

My monkey mind leapt to the death of Jeffrey Henderson, professional protestor and recruiter for Animals First. Why did he try to see the mayor last week? Was it the Shoreline Park issue or did he have other concerns? I figured my chances were slim that the mayor would admit to ever having met with Henderson, let alone tell me the reason for the meeting.

And where the hell was Michelle?

Hands squeezing my shoulders broke my concentration. Alicia rested her chin on top of my head and said, "I got a call. I've got an offering coming in on the Fredricks' house. I hate leaving you with all the mess." She paused. "Pete's in the office. Maybe he could handle this."

Pete was the newest realtor in her office. No way would she ever feel comfortable with him covering her multi-million-dollar sale. I swiveled my chair to face her. "Go. Otherwise, you'd end up on the phone talking Pete through the whole deal."

She looked at me, then at our home phone, and bit her lip.

"Don't worry, honey. I'll be here in case anyone calls. And Keesha has both our cell phone numbers if she needs to reach us."

Alicia's gaze was still focused on the phone. She finally gave my shoulder another quick squeeze as she dashed toward our bedroom. She returned in under five minutes in black linen slacks and a violet shirt, looking like the real estate professional she was. She picked up her purse, gave me a fast smooch, and flew out the door.

I picked up our cordless home phone and wandered out front. Ginger was catnapping on the front porch. I sat beside her and ran my fingers through her thick, silky fur as I considered Michelle and homeless people in general. Something kept telling me that Michelle's absence and the murder at Highland Medical were related, but I couldn't see how. She'd have to be in Hench's lab to witness the murder. What would she be doing there? And if, against all odds, she did see the murder, how did she get away without anyone spotting her? If she came across Sloan's dead body, why didn't she call the police instead of running? As far as I could see, the only scenario that explained everything would have Michelle killing Sloan, for reasons unknown, and going on the run. It wasn't a possibility I was willing to raise with Alicia.

To prevent my thoughts from spiraling further downward, I turned to my nascent idea regarding the city buying or renting empty warehouses or even abandoned houses and converting them to care services and residential areas for the homeless. I called the city manager, the head of the redevelopment agency for the city, and the director of an agency that sheltered battered women to hear their thoughts on the issue. By the time I heard their widely differing points of view, I'd fleshed out several details.

After patting Ginger one last time, I went into the house and pounded out my proposal on the computer. I stopped only when Ginger showed up in my office yowling insistently. She thought nothing of stalking across my keyboard if I dared try to ignore her.

To quiet my insistent furry friend, I gave her a snack of grain-free, ocean whitefish treats. I stood in the kitchen and stared at the silent phone, worried about breaking my promise to Alicia to keep guard over it. But I figured the faster I got this proposal to the council and to staff, the better the chances I could head off the mayor's busing scheme.

I returned to my home office, printed off copies, and hopped into my car. Within fifteen minutes, I stormed into the mayor's office with a counterproposal to investigate renting empty warehouses in the city and creating temporary housing and social services centers for the homeless with some set aside specifically for homeless veterans. I felt an amazing sense of satisfaction slapping the proposal onto Thompson's desktop. Too bad she wasn't there.

As I placed the papers down, I noticed that Thompson kept an old-fashioned weekly appointment book, apparently in addition to the official, online calendar every council member used that was accessible to staff so they could make appointments for constituents. The book was open on her desk. I glanced at it to see where she was today. No surprise that she was attending a fraternal club meeting whose members, I knew, comprised most of the business leaders in the city. Curiosity got the better of me. I flipped back a page to see if she met with any of those people before coming up with her busing plan for the homeless. A few prominent names appeared and some names that seemed like they should mean something to me, but the file drawer in my memory bank wouldn't open to provide me background. I gave another brief thought to talking to my doctor about my memory during my next heart appointment. Of course, if I remembered to do that, I probably didn't have much to worry about.

I was about to close Thompson's book when I noticed that one appointment was whited out. I held the page up to the light, but I couldn't see through the liquid coverage. Then I turned the page over and looked at the indented marks made by Thompson's writing. No mirror was needed to read the backwards script. This was the appointment Carlotti mentioned. The whited-out name was clearly Jeffery Henderson, the man who shot Thompson with the paintball. I checked the date of the appointment.

Thompson's meeting with Jeffrey Henderson was the day before Henderson broke into the council chamber and shot her with a paintball. He was killed less than a week after that. I wondered if John Johnson, Jr., was on to more than he knew.

Chapter Thirteen

Alicia came home exhausted but upbeat. The offer on the house was a solid one, and she'd be meeting with the sellers Saturday to present it.

Despite all that was going on, or maybe because of it, we decided to invite the whole family to Shabbat dinner. Alicia called Ben and Sarah. Both accepted and Sarah added that Amy and David would be accompanying her as well.

I raised an eyebrow at Alicia. "I wonder why our recalcitrant son-in-law is gracing us with his presence."

Alicia shrugged and began the preparations for beef stew. She browned the meat for the stew as I chopped the onions. I could tell she was mulling over something.

"What's on your mind?"

"David's coming to dinner, and I want you to be nice to him."

"I'm always nice to him." Alicia didn't bother to correct me, so I knew that wasn't the real issue. Heavier things must be weighing on her mind. I slid the minced onions into the frying pan. The aroma made me salivate. I reached in to snag a piece of beef, but Alicia slapped my hand away.

"I need the bell pepper and garlic chopped, too."

"Aye, aye, top chef, ma'am. But while I'm at it, maybe you could tell me what's really bothering you."

"I read an article on AIDS. It's on the rise again because the young guys think it's a controllable disease, not a death sentence."

"Are you worried about Ben?"

"Of course I am. We didn't even think about him turning out to be bisexual when we talked to him about safe sex."

"Considering he never told us about his attraction to men until six months ago, I'm not sure how we could have foreseen this when he was ten and we did the whole birds and bees talk."

"We talked to him about using condoms when he was a teen and started dating Jennifer."

"You did. Not me. Never had a need to use them nor a desire to learn."

Alicia glared at me, and I could tell I wasn't going to score points on this conversation no matter what I said. I sighed and started chopping the peppers.

The house phone rang, interrupting my sous chef attempts. I caught it in the living room where Ginger was napping on the couch. Thompson's unwelcome voice added to my lack of joy.

"What the hell do you think you're doing trying to run a proposal behind my back?"

"Hello, Madam Mayor. How nice of you to call. Which measure are you referring to?"

"What do you mean which measure? The socialist plan for the street people, of course. Where do you think you're going to get the money to remodel and equip those warehouses into Club Meds for indigents?"

"Where were you planning on getting the money for the buses and the share of costs when we ship hundreds of people to Goleta?"

Thompson was silent for several seconds. "Wherever it comes from, it's cheaper than getting into the hotel business for Section 8 loonies."

"The people of this city deserve fair treatment. All of them. And if you think you don't like this proposal for dealing in a humane manner with people, wait until you see my ideas for the animals." I hung up, picked up Ginger, and cuddled her against my chest. Holding my cat was a wise decision, especially when the alternative involved chopping with a knife while furious.

****

At dinner, the subject of sex didn't rear its head. Neither did Zach nor the adoption. Knowing of his sister's disapproval of the whole process probably lessened Ben's desire to broach the topic. I would have argued it out. Ben, like Alicia, tended to be the peacemaker, not the confronter. So, I let it slide.

After dinner, David stepped forward and asked to speak to me, privately. The last time that happened was when he asked for my help in getting Sarah to listen to his marriage proposal. We hadn't talked one-on-one since. In fact, in the last year we avoided each other's company. I couldn't imagine what he wanted to say to me now, but with Alicia's warning about treating him nicely replaying itself in my ear, I agreed.

I watched his bright blue eyes flash around the room as he settled himself in one of my office chairs. The dark of his hair and beard highlighted the jewel tones of those eyes. When I was feeling generous toward him, I thought they were his most attractive feature. The jury was out on how I rated his personal attributes at that moment.

"Sarah told me about Ben. What he wants to do. I know she's not crazy about it." David scooted to the edge of the chair and leaned toward me. "And I understand where she's coming from. I get that she sees this as a betrayal of her father. You see, I was raised with the belief that family is family. That you stick with your family. Support them no matter what."

I tensed. If he was going to try to talk me out of adopting Ben, he'd be leaving this room with a lecture that would turn his ears red.

"That early training is part of the problem. Part of my problem. I don't know if Sarah told you or not, but I've been in therapy for the last year. I'm learning that I can love my father and not agree with him. His opinion on anything is not binding on me. His anger toward you doesn't mean I can't like you. And as much as I love and support Sarah, I don't agree with her about Ben. I think Ben is one lucky guy to be adopted by you. I wanted you to know you have my support."

As I looked into his eyes, I saw an openness and vulnerability I'd seen only once before, when he was afraid that he'd lost Sarah's love. My resistance to him evaporated. I held out my right hand. "Welcome to the family."

****

In bed that night, Alicia cuddled into the curve of my arm. She gently trailed her fingers along my stomach as I reviewed my conversation with David. "He ended up giving me a hug. I was so shocked, I'm not sure I hugged back."

"I'm glad to hear he's in therapy. He's gone through several huge upheavals in his life in the last year. I wonder what he'll tell Sarah about this evening."

"That might be pillow talk worth eavesdropping on." I held Alicia's wandering hand in mine. "How are you doing?"

"My mind keeps leaping back to Michelle. Do you think she knows how to protect herself?"

I squeezed her hand. "Michelle's been on the streets for a lot of years. If you're talking about safe sex, I haven't a clue. If you're talking about survival, I think she'll do fine."

Alicia didn't clarify her question. She merely pecked me on the cheek and rolled to her side. As I spooned against her, I realized it would be another night of little sleep.

Chapter Fourteen

I awoke earlier than usual and wondered if Ginger had jolted the bed while pouncing on my toes. A glimpse down at the foot of the bed revealed an angelic cat with her face tucked into the ball of her body. No disturbance there. And Alicia was curled on her side breathing softly. It didn't seem as if she'd stirred in the last hour, so her movement hadn't awakened me. Then I heard it. The buzz of my phone. I'd put it on vibrate when we went to bed.

I glanced at the screen and saw my son-in-law's name. I punched the button to answer the call.

"I was on my way to take a deposition in Goleta when they announced it on the radio. I figured you might not be up yet, but I wanted to tell you before Alicia heard it."

"Heard what?"

"Some bird watchers found a body near a hiking trail in northern Santa Barbara, the Lauro Canyon Reservoir area. A woman in her fifties. It sounded a lot like how Sarah described her aunt."

I awakened Alicia and broke the news. We both pulled on some clothes and headed out the door where we found David waiting for us in our driveway. Despite our protests, David called another associate to cover the deposition for him so he could accompany us to the police station. Alicia and I sat in the backseat of his Prius holding hands as he assumed the chauffeur role. All three of us spent the trip in silent contemplation.

Detective Levine turned out to be in charge of the case. As I greeted him for the third time in as many crimes, I began to wonder if our police department was severely understaffed. I told the detective about Michelle. He called up the missing person report and reviewed it with us. There weren't many identifying details we could add. She didn't have any visible tattoos that I'd noticed, and nothing else leapt to mind as unusual or unique to her.

"Her gall bladder and tonsils were removed," Alicia said. "The tonsillectomy happened when she was a kid, but the gall bladder was only seven years ago. Arthroscopic, so I doubt the scars would even be noticeable."

I could tell Alicia was reaching for anything that might make a difference. The way Detective Levine thanked us for the information made me suspect we hadn't helped much.

"How long has the woman been dead?" I asked, thinking about the timing of Michelle's disappearance.

"Our preliminary estimate is two to three days."

I realized that, unfortunately, Michelle's disappearance fit into that time frame.

From the police station, David drove us to a local coffee shop for a late breakfast. He twirled a fork between his fingers as we waited for our order to be delivered. "Did you hear the guys on the phones beside us? They were fielding calls all the time we were there from other people thinking that the...uh, lady might be someone they know."

I figured he was trying to spare our feelings by not saying "dead body."

Alicia sipped some coffee. "It probably happens every time they find an unidentified body. That never even crossed my mind before. But now I keep wondering. If she's not Michelle, who could she be? What other family is going through this kind of hell?"

The detective had intimated that the usual identifiers of fingerprints and dental records were not in play in this case. He didn't go into details as to why. Unfortunately, that left it to my lurid imagination. I could only hope Alicia's mind didn't travel down the same dark path. "He made it clear that there wouldn't even be a tentative identification until after the autopsy. Even then, it might come down to DNA evidence."

David dropped the fork on the table. "God, I hope not. That could take weeks."

If even then, I thought, but kept that suspicion to myself.

****

"What are you doing here?" Sarah asked David when we entered the house. "I thought you were at a deposition."

"More to the point, what are you doing here?" I asked. "Isn't this your Saturday to be at the law firm?"

"I am. Or I was. But I think I've got a line on who made the appointment for Jeffrey Henderson. I had a no-show for a nine o'clock appointment this morning. Turns out the name was fake, or, at least, no one is admitting that someone by that name works there. But there were two contact numbers for it. One was for Animals First and the other for Highland Medical."

"What name did they give?" I asked.

"That's the funny thing. It was a woman's name." Sarah dug through her purse and extracted a file card with today's date and the nine o'clock time written on it. The name on the card was Greer Olaf.

"What makes you think this was the appointment that Henderson had?"

"Only two people have skipped appointments in the six months I've been on the job. I was easily able to contact both of them and reschedule. But I called both the numbers on the card, and nobody at either place knew a Greer Olaf. I've never run into a bogus name and contact number before."

I flipped the card over and saw it was stamped. "What's this?"

Sarah glanced at the card. "That's the date the appointment was made. It's two days before Henderson broke into the council meeting."

Alicia patted Sarah on the shoulder as she passed by. "That's all terribly interesting, but I have to go lie down." She headed for the bedroom.

Sarah frowned. "What's with Mom?" She turned to David and asked again, "And what are you doing here?"

I left David the task of filling Sarah in on the news. I followed Alicia instead and found her sitting on the edge of the bed, head in her hands. I knelt beside her. "I'm not giving up on finding Michelle alive."

When Alicia raised her head, I saw the tears in her eyes. I handed her a tissue. She wiped her face and blew her nose. "I'm not giving up either. Mom and Dad would never forgive me if I did." She squared her shoulders and stood. "I need to go into the office for the presentation of the offer. After that, I'm going to check out the rest of the abandoned houses on my list. I should be home by noon."

I watched her stride toward the shower to get ready for her day. I never felt so helpless in my life.

****

After the kids and Alicia left, Ginger and I settled into my office. Determined to do something to help ease the pain in Alicia's heart, I set to work. Emails were first. I shot one off to Sophia Carlotti asking to meet with her to discuss a proposal to deal with the ground squirrels and another to Highland Medical's public relations department asking for an appointment to discuss the expansion they were planning. Neither of these were the real reason for the contact, but I saw no other path to breach their respective resistance to my real line of inquiry.

Next, I called Michelle's employers. After verifying that they were open, I headed for the offices of Premier Cleaning Services. I asked to see Michelle's supervisor.

Gordon Bates sported a luxuriant mustache that he groomed with his right hand whenever he seemed to be thinking. Since he carefully considered his answers to every one of my questions before speaking, his mustache got a workout.

"You realize we cannot give any personal information about our employees, even if you are a relative."

"Yes, I know. What I'm after is more how your operation works. For example, are your employees expected to transport themselves to their worksites or does the company offer a van?"

Bates tugged at the tip of his mustache for a moment before answering. "On occasion, the company provides a van for jobs that are out of town. Anything in Santa Barbara, the employees are expected to arrange for their own transportation."

"So, Michelle and her coworkers all arrived at the Highland Medical facility independently. And they would leave the same way."

"I imagine a few might carpool, but that's up to them."

"Highland Medical has all kinds of experiments going on. I'm sure they wouldn't want just anyone wandering through their facility. Do you screen your employees?"

Bates's fingers increased their speed. "Our employees are bonded."

By whom? I wondered, since I knew Michelle had a police record. Minor things, but I thought they would be enough to disqualify her for a bond. "Do your workers wear anything to identify themselves as Premier Cleaning Services employees?"

"Absolutely. They all have uniforms that they must wear on the job."

Michelle wasn't wearing the uniform the time she met us for dinner. "Do you have a changing room here for them to use?"

"Employees come to work in their uniforms. Many of the companies have lockers where workers can store their personal belongings while they work, but none that I know of provide changing rooms. The crews learn what is available for them because they work at the same place Monday through Friday. A different crew takes over on the weekend."

"They check in here before they go to their assignments and then check in when they are through?"

"Yes. Well, mostly. The business office runs seven days a week, but it closes at 8 p.m. and doesn't open until 5 a.m. Occasionally, workers may have to work later than that or leave earlier."

"So, when Michelle didn't report in that night, no one worried."

"They noted it in the log, but, no, no one called out the dogs." He gave a weak chuckle. "There's more of a concern if someone doesn't show up for a shift than if they fail to sign out afterward."

"How often are your employees paid?"

"Every two weeks."

"Michelle wouldn't have received a check yet, then."

"No. She'd need to complete at least a week with us before she would get a check."

That confirmed my thought that Michelle must not have very much cash to be living on. "Have any employees ever complained about their treatment at Highland?"

"Never."

"Has Highland expressed any displeasure with your company's work?"

"Minor items. But whenever we get any complaints from our customers, they are dealt with immediately. That's why our company is so successful. Premier Cleaning Services has been in business for seventy-three years, and we've built a reputation for honest, hard labor using the safest, most-effective, green materials available."

"So, when Highland complained about the cleaning crew fogging up the lens of their security cameras..."

Bates lifted a file that lay in front of him and flipped through the pages. "You must be mistaken. I would have heard about something like that, and there's no record of such a complaint being made."

Chapter Fifteen

When I returned to my car, I checked my emails and found a reply from Carlotti as well as Highland Medical. I texted Carlotti that I'd meet her in ten minutes. I emailed Highland and set the appointment for an hour and a half from now. I hoped that would give me both time for travel and time to wheedle information from Carlotti.

Carlotti's dark eyes glared at me from across her desk. When my first questions concerned her connection with Dr. Sloan and the members of Animals First, she growled at me. "There's no way I'm giving you our membership list. The police needed to get a court order before I gave it to them. You'll have to do the same. And good luck with that. And why are you asking all this? Are you related to Sloan or something? I thought you were here about the ground squirrels. If not, the door is behind you."

I handed over the draft of my proposal. While she read through it, I stood and wandered around the small office. Several framed *Santa Barbara News Press* articles hung on the wall. One proclaimed the founding of Animals First and displayed a picture of homeless kittens rather than one of the board of directors or the founder. I found that to be in character for the antisocial Carlotti. Another one showed a protest march at Shoreline Park that Animals First organized. A few local dignitaries marched along with the protesters. A color photo drew me to the next article. It detailed the organization's successful rescue of a mountain lion orphaned by the wildfires that consumed the hills above Santa Barbara four years before. The photo was of a group of volunteers gathered around a trap from which the recovered cat was being released back into the wild. A tall blonde stood in the back row. I squinted, trying to make out her features, but all the people were looking down at the fleeing cougar.

"Do you have the original of this photograph?" I asked

Carlotti, jolting her out of her perusal of my proposal.

She glared at me. "Why would I? The newspaper guy took it, not me. Why are you interested, anyway?"

I tapped my finger on the photo. "This looks like my sister-in-law."

"Don't touch that," she snapped. She limped her way over to the picture. Her eyes followed my finger to the back row of people, then she glanced at me. "What's her name?"

"Michelle. Michelle Mazer."

"Not her."

"She sometimes goes by Shelly. She's missing and we're trying to find any leads we can about her."

"Still not her." Carlotti reached across the desk and hefted the papers I'd given her. "You did a pretty decent job with the proposal. Not exactly the methods I would have chosen, but I guess you'd lose your job if you suggested everyone on the Mesa move out of their homes and close the cliffs to the public." She handed me the proposal. "Good luck finding your sister-in-law. It's a dangerous world for women."

****

I wished I could head straight to the offices of the *News Press*, but I barely had time to make my appointment with the PR representative at Highland Medical. I tried to make an appointment with Dr. Olsson first, but the call went through to voice mail. I wanted to find out more from her regarding why Sloan was in Hench's lab, what might have been delivered that night to the loading dock, and whether a cleaning crew member would be involved in some way with unloading those animals or supplies. With no Olsson around, I decided to make do with the public relations department.

I was swept into a regal office as soon as I arrived. The pale-green walls of the public relations team displayed pictures of the gleaming exterior of the research lab as well as renderings of the shiny labs and busy scientists. One engraved, brass plaque listed the two patents held by the company. The empty space on the plaque seemed to promise a multitude of additions to this honor roll.

Josh Robbins offered me a seat. "I'm glad we could accommodate your request to come in today. Our department isn't usually operating on a Saturday, but it's been a rather, um, unusual week." He cleared his throat. "I understand you have some questions about our proposed new facility."

"I do. But I was also wondering if I could speak to one of the scientists who is currently doing research. I met a Dr. Olsson when I was here last. Could I speak with her?"

"I'm afraid that won't be possible. Dr. Olsson resigned from Highland."

"Resigned? Why?"

He cleared his throat again. "I'm afraid I'm not allowed to discuss personnel matters."

"I understand. But, as a councilperson, I would have concerns if a senior scientist at this firm decided, say, something egregious was occurring here. So egregious that she couldn't stay on staff."

Robbins frowned. "Oh, no. It was nothing like that." He hesitated, looking pained, then spit out, "Dr. Olsson was offered a job with another company as a head researcher. I imagine they were impressed by her success here at Highland."

"What company? And please don't tell me you can't say. The only way I'll feel comfortable with Dr. Olsson's decision to leave here is if I speak with her myself." I watched him squirm and decided to play the politics card. "I'd hate to bring my reservations to the other council members right before Highland brings their proposed expansion up for a vote."

"Perhaps Dr. Hench could tell you more."

"Perhaps. But I'm talking with you." His silence continued, so I picked up one of his business cards from the holder on his desk and stood. "I'm sorry I wasted your time. I'll let the City Council know about the level of your cooperation."

Before I reached the door, Robbins called out, "She got a job with Exeter Research. A biotech facility in the Bay area."

I turned around and sat back down. "Thank you. Now let's discuss your plans for expansion."

****

"The police let us do a full day of work yesterday," Ben said when I returned home. "I actually got assigned a locker and my lab section." He crunched on a carrot stick. The crumbs of a sandwich littered his plate.

"Too bad they don't feed you there."

"This is a snack. I'm going out for lunch."

"Friend or new squeeze?" I clamped down on the additional question as to the sex of the individual.

"We'll find out." He gave a cheeky smirk.

I checked the answering machine. No messages. "Were there any calls?"

"Nope. Expecting someone?"

"I'm hoping the investigator we hired might have some news on your aunt."

"How's Mom holding up with that?"

I figured he would hear from his sister at some point about the unidentified woman's body, so I filled him in on that.

His face lost its habitual grin on the news. "Poor Mom."

I pulled up a chair to our new glass-topped kitchen table. I'd complained to Alicia before we bought it that viewing my bare feet while eating could destroy my appetite. She sweetly informed me that if that was the case, maybe it would help me drop the weight I was always complaining about. I hate it when she wins an argument. "Tell me about Highland Medical."

Ben launched into a detailed account of people and labs, procedures and equipment, half of which was Greek to me. But he regained his smile as he spoke, so I hoped this assignment would work out well for him.

"They even have a full gym in the basement that we can use. And they have a machine shop for maintenance. If we need to modify a piece of equipment for an experiment, we can request the change and the guys downstairs whip it out. Very rad. Made me think about installing something like that in the corner of my basement."

"Do you have a clue how to operate any of that equipment?"

"Nope. But how hard could it be?" He finished the sandwich. "Everybody was talking about Dr. Sloan and his murder and all. I'll be working with one of Sloan's assistants, Caleb." Ben rushed on. "Not where Sloan was murdered or anything. We work in a different part of the building."

Ben's hurried explanation made me realize he noticed my horrified expression. I got myself under control. "What were they saying about him?"

"Caleb said Sloan was a good guy. Some docs make you work extra hours and weekends. But not Sloan. He said Sloan ran a sane lab. No drama over assignments. Everyone helped with the clean-up. No favorites. No late hours. He closed it at five so everyone could get home for dinner. Talked about how important it was to spend time with your family. Caleb told me that Sloan's wife left him because he used to be in the lab at all hours. Never came home. Guess that made him change his ways."

"Seems like a case of too little, too late if he was trying to save his marriage."

Ben shrugged and waved a carrot stick at me. "Want one? It's healthy. Mom won't be mad at you for snacking on these."

"Thanks." I took it and crunched for a moment as I considered the gentle man in front of me. "How do you feel about using animals as test subjects?"

"I don't know. I won't be working directly with the animals. I'm in the pharm lab. I'll be mixing up the medications, not administering them. I don't think I could do that." He wiped his mouth and pushed his empty plate away. "I know important breakthroughs have come because of these tests. And I know that a lot of the researchers try hard to treat the animals well. In fact, Caleb told me that Dr. Sloan made sure everyone in his lab took good care of the animals. But I'm pretty sure I won't end up working in a place like Highland. I'm too much of a softy. Don't tell my sister that." Ben winked. "Speaking of sis, here's another factoid. Did you know they only use male rats and mice for the tests since the scientists don't want to factor in the hormonal swings in females? Makes you wonder if any of these meds are really good for women."

"It does, indeed." I thought of Michelle and her struggles with the drugs prescribed for her. "Did anyone say anything about the cleaning crew that works there?"

"Not that I remember. Dr. Hench might have talked about them when he did the orientation, but since I'm mainly working in the mornings and they come late afternoon, I didn't pay much attention."

"You met Hench?"

"Yep. He's not only a researcher, he's like some big office manager for the company."

I leaned back in my chair and stared at the tips of my shoes through the glass. A flash of memory struck my brain. Kyle Hench, spokesperson and company fixer, was one of the names on Mayor Thompson's calendar for the previous week.

"By the way," Ben said as he rinsed his empty dish and put it in the dishwasher. "I know you said you'd look into it, but I talked with a family attorney. The one my friend's dads used for his adoption. I made an appointment for Monday so we could discuss all the issues, but she thought it should be a straightforward procedure. It'll be you and me and Mom. I hope you don't mind that I went ahead and contacted the attorney without you."

"I don't mind at all. I'm sorry I dropped the ball."

Ben gave a wry smile. "Seems you've been a little busy."

I wanted to envelop him in a massive hug and never let go. I refrained. Barely.

"You sure you still want to do this, what with Zach getting in your face and all?" His voice held an echo of doubt that made my heart ache.

Visions of newborn Ben flashed through my mind. He was squirmy and covered in bodily fluids, as I held him so the doctors could cut his umbilical cord. I fell in love with him at that moment, and nothing in the intervening twenty plus years changed that. "Yes, son, I very much want to do this."

****

Alicia arrived home a little past noon. I told her about Ben, Highland Medical, and the picture in the *News Press* article while we ate lunch. "I'm going to head over to the

News Press office and track down the original of that photo."

"Why is a possible picture of Michelle so important? What if she was in Santa Barbara four years ago? How would that help us now?"

"If she was here and volunteering with Animals First, that would mean she was functional at that point. Which means she might have made friends in the area. Friends she might be staying with."

Alicia tucked her purse under her arm. "In that case, you have yourself a research assistant for the afternoon."

A quick check on the internet informed us that the micro-fiche copies of all the *News Press* articles were housed on the second floor of the city's main library rather than at the paper itself. So, we headed to Anapamu Street and found parking in the garage next to the library. A wide staircase led from the main floor of the library to a balcony where the microfiche and viewers were located. The library owned only two view-ing machines, but both were available. A librarian helped us get started searching the file drawers for the correct time period. Since the wildfire mentioned in the article started in June of that year, Alicia took June through August while I concentrated on September through December. Alicia looked for any stories regarding Animal First activities while I skimmed for the photo.

Alicia struck gold first with a story of the rescue of the mountain lion by Animal First volunteers. Unfortunately, the only picture was of the wild cat, and the volunteers quoted in the article did not include Michelle. The only person mentioned that we recognized was the late, paintball-toting Jeffrey Henderson in his role as volunteer and community outreach coordinator. He spoke eloquently of the fact that not just people lost their homes when fires ravaged the hillsides. Animals, too, lost homes and families to the blaze. He explained that the organization included various volunteers who had expertise in animal care including a veterinarian, a scientist, and a former National Park ranger. Thus, his confidence in the group's ability to successfully care for, and eventual release, the mountain lion.

Buoyed by Alicia's find, I scrolled onward. I finally

found the photo that hung on Sophia Carlotti's wall. It was from a story published in October of that year. The copy on the film was smaller and blurrier than the framed one I'd seen. I enlarged it as much as possible and showed it to Alicia. She agreed that the woman might have a resemblance to Michelle, but we'd need the original to know for sure.

I showed my find to the librarian, and he suggested we call the *News Press* offices for the contact information for the photographer. Unfortunately, the office staff of the newspaper didn't seem to keep weekend hours since my call went unanswered. I briefly considered calling John Johnson for the information, but I didn't trust him. I added a reminder to stop by the offices Monday to my already long to-do list.

As tired as I was, I was glad to see that the afternoon's excursion seemed to encourage Alicia. As soon as we returned home, she pulled up her real estate listings and started making a new list of places to investigate.

The doorbell rang. Our private investigator, Keesha Collins, stood on the front step. Her face was grim.

I escorted her into the living room and hustled off to pry Alicia away from her maps and GPS. We sat down together on the sofa, holding hands, my eyes glued to Collins, who sat opposite us on an upholstered chair.

Collins opened her phone and scrolled to a page. "I followed up on the information you gave me on the homeless groups at Rattlesnake Canyon and at Gutierrez Park. Two people confirm the young girl's story of Michelle being in the Rattlesnake Canyon camp that night and being told to leave. In addition, one of the people at the warehouse on Gutierrez claimed that a woman matching Michelle's description came to their encampment very late Tuesday night after everyone was bedded down. Lefty and the woman talked for a while. My informant fell asleep at that point. When he woke up the next morning, the woman wasn't in camp."

Alicia sat up straight. "So, Lefty lied to us."

"It seems so."

I asked, "Did you talk with Lefty?"

"No. Soon after the two of you visited there, Lefty took all of his belongings and left as well. He seems to have disappeared."

Chapter Sixteen

"There's more." Collins leaned forward. "After you made your second visit to the warehouse, a man showed up there. He also asked about Michelle. He flashed a photo of her and offered a reward for information. My guy thought the man was armed."

"Police?" Alicia asked.

Collins shook her head. "I doubt it. He didn't produce a badge, and the police don't usually wave money as an incentive to talk."

I thought of Johnson. "Maybe a reporter?"

"Maybe. But they're not known for their overly generous ways, either."

"Did any of the people at the camp give them information?" I asked.

"No. Before Lefty took off, he asked the group not to talk to anyone looking for him or anyone else that might have stayed at their camp. They're all pretty loyal to him. The guy who talked to me only did so because he was worried about Lefty's safety." Collins looked at each of us in turn. "Maybe Michelle had another reason for leaving L.A. other than to visit you."

We sat in silence for several moments before Alicia whispered, "The gun. She carried that before any of this started."

"She warned us to stop looking for her or *they* will find her," I said. "Maybe she isn't as delusional as we thought."

Collins asked, "Did she mention anything that happened in L.A.? Any trouble at all?"

"No," Alicia said. "She wasn't in Los Angeles long. She was there trying to find us. The last place she spent time in was San Diego."

Collins slipped her phone into her pocket and stood. "I know how hard it is for you to sit and wait for me to do my job, but I think it would be better if you two didn't do any more investigating on your own. I don't know who this guy is who's after Michelle, but it may be dangerous. I'd hate to lose my clients before they pay the final bill."

****

"What kind of shit has Michelle gotten herself into?" Alicia sounded angry, frustrated, and scared all at the same time. I could relate on all fronts.

"I have no idea. Or maybe too many ideas and not enough facts. And now I'm concerned for everyone's safety. Are you still thinking of visiting those abandoned houses?"

"No. I'll send the list to Keesha."

I sighed with relief. "Guess our job is to wait and see what happens."

"Actually, I was thinking of taking a little field trip to San Diego. It's awfully nice there in the fall."

I groaned. "What part of 'dangerous and guns' did you not hear?"

"The part where my sister might be safe from all of that. I don't want her to be the dead body they found. Until I know for sure she's not, I'm not going to be okay."

"So, you're going to put yourself in danger to make sure Michelle isn't?"

"I'll be fine. I'm merely going to chat with people at the shelter she told us about and see if I can find the company she worked for."

I mulled that over for a few minutes. "Okay. Pack your bags. I'll call Ben and have him take care of Ginger while we're gone."

"No. You're not going. You have the City Council and your massage appointments. Plus, we need someone here in case something breaks."

"We have the appointment with the adoption attorney Monday afternoon."

"I'll be back before then."

"At least take Ben with you. He can share the driving, and he's big enough to be intimidating."

"You think I'm going to bring my son into this mess?"

My voice took on an edge of anger. "You just said you weren't going to be doing anything dangerous. You can't have it both ways."

Alicia's eyes flashed a warning. But, then, she took a deep breath and said, "Fine. I'll call Ben and see if he's free." She put up a finger. "But if he's not, I'm still going. By myself." She stomped out of the living room.

****

I fancied that Ginger and I were getting used to being alone together in the house. Alicia unbent enough to kiss me goodbye before they left. She also promised to call several times a day. Ben swore he would make sure she did. The only thing left to do was give them both the most protective hug I could.

I felt a need to be physical and changed into my gym clothes and headed off for a workout. I thought I might run into Quentin while I was there, but instead of the judge, I saw Highland Medical's own Dr. Kyle Hench on one of the rowing machines. Although rowing was not one of my usual exercises, I saw that the universe provided an empty machine next to Hench, so I took it.

As I strapped my feet into the pedals, I looked over at Hench. "I didn't know you belonged to this gym."

Hench did a double take. I saw it in his eyes when he placed me, and his frown of concentration morphed into the professional smile as he stopped rowing. "I'm here mainly in the evenings, but I missed a couple of sessions this week. As you can well imagine."

"That explains it. I'm mainly a morning person, but I got antsy and decided to put in an extra workout."

We took simultaneous swigs from our water bottles.

"Are things calming down at Highland? Are the police still there?"

"Unfortunately, we may be having a police presence for some time. I'm sure you understand that I'd like to get back into my lab." His eyes lit up. "Perhaps if you put in a word…"

I shook my head. "Sorry. I have no sway over the police.

They go out of their way to show no favoritism to council members. Were you able to get the lab animals back?"

"Not yet. The Humane Society is still fighting us. I don't suppose you can help us out with that either."

I shook my head again. "I heard a suspect was detained by the police. A Sophia Carlotti?"

"Yes. One of the animal rights enthusiasts. More heart than brains, I'm afraid. But she held a vendetta against Nathan, that's for sure. She wrote letters threatening almost all of us. Still, I don't know why she picked Sloan. I'd think there were at least ten people ahead of him on her hit list, me being at the top."

"Maybe it was bad luck on his part. After all, he was shot in your lab, not his own. Maybe she got the two of you confused."

Hench's eyes flew open wide.

"Oh, sorry. Thinking out loud. Probably not a good thing to do. I'm sure the police would have warned you if you were in any danger." I pulled on the handles of the rowing machine a few times. When Hench didn't respond, I said, "I heard she got into the lab through the door that opened onto the loading dock."

He wiped his face. "For someone on the wrong side of the police, you seem to have a good source of information."

I shrugged and started to row again. "During my tour through Highland, you told me the only people who possessed the keys to those doors were you, the facilities manager, and the head of security. Since none of you were there, I thought my source must be mistaken about that bit of the story."

Hench clenched his water bottle and towel. "I'll let you get on with your workout."

As I watched him leave the room, I wondered what other lies were part of his Highland Medical spiel.

****

By Sunday morning, I'd heard from Alicia three times: once to tell me they arrived, once after her visit to the shelter and the police, and once in the morning to let me know their plans for the day. I still wasn't happy about them digging into Michelle's past down in San Diego, but I knew Alicia was determined. And a determined Alicia was a frightening force of nature.

I drove over to Sarah's house and picked up Amy for my usual Sunday morning babysitting gig. After packing my car with all the gear a four-month-old needs to survive a few hours outside her normal environment, I strapped Amy into her safety seat and indulged in a little car stereo karaoke on the way back to our house.

I took Amy into our backyard and set up her enclosed and shaded playpen. Once she was contentedly chewing on her stuffed bunny, I sat beside her with my laptop and started communicating with staff about Tuesday's upcoming City Council meeting and the proposals I hoped to get on the agenda. The whole time I kept checking for messages from Alicia, Ben, Collins, or Michelle. Nothing. However, a text came through from an unknown number.

Heard sis-in-law missing. Want help? -JJ Jr.

I tapped my phone against my leg as questions bounced around my mind. How was the reporter able to get my cell phone number? How did he know about Michelle? Why would he offer to help?

I was about to delete the text when a better question came to me, namely, could he help?

Before I could decide what to do, another text appeared.

Have more info on Highland.

I took the bait and called.

"Listen," Johnson said. "When I talked with Jeff Henderson, he told me he'd tried to see a Dr. Kyle Hench at Highland Medical. Is that name familiar to you?"

"Yes."

"Jeff got thrown out on his ear. But he kept calling Hench several times a day. Hench finally took his call and agreed to meet with him."

"When was this?"

"A few days before he died. I don't know if they ever met, but I know Jeff wanted to talk to the guy about more than the use of animals in research."

"Like what?"

"He wasn't clear. But he mentioned Sloan, the guy who was killed, and another researcher, Dr. Olsson. Do you know them?"

"I've met Olsson, but not Sloan."

"Any ideas why Jeff wanted to talk with Hench about those two?"

"Sorry. Can't help you. But you mentioned help finding my sister-in-law. What did you have in mind?"

"I go all over the city, and I've developed a lot of contacts. If you gave me a current picture of Michelle, I could check with my people and see if anything pops."

And I was sure I'd be seeing that photo in the *News Press* rather than the old DMV picture. "Thanks, but we already have people on that." I hung up before he could ask anything more. I hoped I hadn't given him any quotes that he could mash into a lurid story of political intrigue. I regretted my impulse to call.

****

By afternoon, I was happy to hand Amy back over to her mother and be on my way to Red Boyle's estate for our weekly massage appointment.

"C'mon in," Red yelled when I knocked on the door. She was lying on the couch, an ice pack on her hip. "Glad you're here. That quack of a doctor at the ER wanted me to get a CT scan to make sure nothing else was hurt. Had the nerve to say that at my age we have to be careful. Told him the x-ray was enough. I didn't need any more tests. I've got plenty of padding on my hip. Since there are no broken bones, ice, rest, and a good massage will fix me right back up."

"Now what did you do?" I asked while mentally reviewing the list of contraindicators for a massage. A broken bone was certainly one.

"Tripped. Forgot to watch going down the stairs when the dogs are around."

"You're sure your femur isn't cracked or broken? No fracture to your hip or pelvis?"

"Pfft. A bruise. You set up your table, and then you can help me up onto it."

"Guess this will cut down on your protest marches for a while," I said as I unzipped my cover and pulled out the table.

"Don't you worry. I'll be at the City Council meeting Tuesday. A whole group of us are going to raise Cain about the insanity of increasing the size of that Highland Medical facility when the toxic wastes they already spew out are going into the ground and water."

"How did you hear about the expansion?"

"I have my ways, missy. Did you know your precious mayor is in the hip pocket of the Highland people? They were the largest contributors to her campaign. You never hear about it because they funneled the money through a shady PAC, but our MEAP team is checking into the finances of everybody concerned with that company. We're going to catch 'em with their britches down. And don't you think for one moment you're off the hot seat about poisoning the ground squirrels either."

I extended the wooden legs of the table and flipped it upright. "You'll be glad to know I'm introducing a proposal to study a variety of nonlethal ways of dealing with the squirrels."

"Study? You've got to move on this. This is going to spread up the food chain. People will be dying."

I attached the head rest, smoothed the sheets, and laid out the bolster and the massage oils. "Let's worry about getting you up and around first. Then we can save the world together."

Chapter Seventeen

First thing Monday morning, I called the *News Press* front desk to find out the name and contact information for their photographer. I was right in my assumption that they only used a few, and the receptionist readily gave me the two names. I called both. One remembered taking the shot. He promised to check his files and see what information he could give me.

In the meantime, I decided to check with Dr. Olsson and find out why she left Highland Medical and if she would be willing to share any information on the company. I looked up the website for Exeter Medical, her new employer. It showed no online listing of employees, but it did give a contact phone number.

The person who answered the phone was polite, but clear. No Dr. Olsson worked at their facility. I asked to speak with the human resources department. They confirmed no record existed regarding the hire of one Dr. Olsson or anyone else from Highland Medical.

I drummed my fingers on my desktop for a few moments before sliding open my desk drawer and extracting the business card of Highland Medical's public relations representative. Josh Robbins took my call but expressed amazement when I informed him that Exeter never heard of Ingrid Olsson. He promised to check with HR and get right back to me. I was pleased when I got a return phone call in under ten minutes.

Robbins said, "I talked with our human resources manager, and she told me that Dr. Olsson sent her resignation notice by email. She showed me a copy, and it clearly says that Dr. Olsson was leaving because of having the opportunity of a new position at Exeter and she was sorry for not giving us advance notice, but they needed her up there right away."

"Why would she lie about that?" I asked.

He sounded as puzzled as I was. "I don't have a clue."

"Was the email sent from her home computer or her phone?"

"It shows the message coming from her phone. Why? Does that make a difference?"

"I don't know." I chewed on the information for a moment before thanking Robbins and hanging up.

Why would Ingrid Olsson lie about her new job? Was she cutting ties? Was she hiding her tracks so someone wouldn't be able to find her?

It sounded depressingly like Michelle.

I checked the white pages online. The only Ingrid Olsson listed in Santa Barbara was shown to be seventy years old. I tried the number anyway, but the man who answered assured me that his mother never earned a doctorate, nor were any of his relatives biological research scientists.

Undaunted, I called upon my trusty secret weapon, the best paralegal in my old firm. I phoned Lily and outlined my request to track down the elusive Dr. Olsson.

"You know I've got real work to do, don't you, boss? The stuff they pay me to do? This will cost you lunch next time you're in town. But if you promise to throw in dessert, I might push your job up the line a notch or two."

After agreeing to the extra bribe, I called Alicia. She picked up on the second ring. She and Ben were having a late breakfast at the hotel restaurant. Clanking of utensils and dishes provided the backdrop for our conversation.

"The police say there were no robberies or other crimes during the week or so before Michelle left the area. At least not ones they are actively pursuing. Of course, if Michelle got involved with a drug deal gone bad, the police probably don't even know about it."

I agreed. "Any luck with her former employer?"

"We have an appointment with the HR rep in half an hour. After that, we're going to check one more time with some of the residents of the homeless shelter. Two women who are supposed to be good friends with Michelle will be there later this morning. Then, I guess, we'll head home."

"I'll have a snack ready for you both. I don't want Ben to

look starved and abused when we meet with the adoption attorney."

My phone beeped to indicate another call on the line, so I signed off by sending both of them my love before answering the other call. It was the photographer from the *News Press.*

"Well," he said, "I've got good news and bad. Good news is I found the photo. Bad news is, it's not your sister-in-law in the picture."

"You're sure?"

"Real sure. Got the names on the sheet I file with each photo. I write down the date, the subject, the location, and the names of anyone in the photo. Unless it's a photo of a crowd or something. But this was a staged picture of the Animals First group, so I got all their names. And the tall blonde wasn't Michelle Mazer, but a woman by the name of Dr. Ingrid Olsson."

My mind flashed to my meeting with Olsson. She was tall and slim like Michelle, and her hair color was similar. I now realized the resemblance. But it hadn't occurred to me that a Highland research scientist would be helping to rehabilitate an injured mountain lion. And a member of Animals First also happened to be the lab partner of the murdered scientist? All interesting little facts that Carlotti neglected to mention.

I checked the time. Six hours before the appointment with the adoption attorney, and Alicia and Ben wouldn't be home for at least another five hours. Plenty of time for me to corner Carlotti.

A phone call to Animals First got kicked to an already full message box. A quick check of an online directory did not reveal a home address, or any listing, for Carlotti.

Momentarily stymied, I ran down what I knew of her. I figured privacy rights wouldn't allow me to access any of her information via Veteran's Affairs. But her animal rights involvement could yield results.

I called Sean Gregory, the head of the Humane Society. He sounded pleased to hear from me, perhaps because he and Highland were still stuck in a legal quagmire over the test animals.

"Sean, do you know Sophia Carlotti?"

"Sure. We've worked with Animals First several times to host adoption fairs all over the city."

"Do you have any personal contact information for her? The Animals First office seems to be closed, and I need to talk with her regarding a proposal I'm working on for the City Council."

"The only phone numbers I have are for the office and for our contact, Jeff. Maybe you've heard, but he was killed a week or so ago, so I don't think that number will help you."

"You worked with Jeffrey?"

"Yeah. Great guy. Very organized and easy to work with. I was really upset to hear that he died. We'd begun plans on a campaign to educate people on the stupidity of raising exotic animals as pets, except we didn't exactly use that term in the publicity materials."

"Why exotic animals?"

"Because the idiots who thought it was so swanky to walk their ferrets on leashes seem to be moving to more upscale wildlife, like snow leopards, to impress their friends. It's bad enough that jerks around the world think ground-up rhino horn will make them virile, now we have zillionaires who think their lives aren't complete without their own private, and highly illegal, zoos," Sean muttered. "Goddamn idiots say they're helping save endangered species. Instead, they're increasing demand for poachers to profit from stealing these animals from the wild. Jeff and I joked about setting up our own safari, only our targets would be the wild animal hunters and poachers. After this whole mess with Highland, I might add medical researchers to the hit list."

Chapter Eighteen

"You'll never guess what we found out," Ben said, bounding in the back door and heading straight to the table. He grabbed one of the sandwiches I'd made and an apple. He munched away, leaving Alicia to fill me in.

She picked up her own sandwich but started her report before consuming her late lunch. "We actually learned a few things. One, Michelle held her job in San Diego for eleven months before she gave her notice. During that time, everyone agreed that she'd been highly functional and faithfully taking her new meds. Her girlfriends swear Michelle wasn't involved in any illegal drug use."

Ben swallowed then piped in. "They even said she got on their case when they smoked a joint."

Alicia took over again. "Which makes her being part of a drug deal seem less likely. Her friends had no idea why anyone from San Diego would be looking for her. They didn't think she was in trouble at all."

"Except for her boyfriend," Ben said.

"Boyfriend?" I asked.

"That's the other piece of news. Evidently, Michelle hadn't been living at the shelter the last eight months. She was sharing an apartment with this boyfriend. He got into occasional trouble with other homeless people. Michelle's girlfriends said he'd always stick up for the underdog and that got him into a few fights. Some where the police got involved. Anyway, he left town suddenly two months ago. According to her friends, Michelle was heartbroken. She decided to start again somewhere new, which is when she quit her job and tried to find us."

"So, she wasn't trying to follow him?"

"They didn't think so because she didn't know where he went. But the most interesting thing is that the boyfriend was an ex-military sergeant by the name of Lefty."

"Son of a... I don't suppose it's a coincidence."

"Their description of him fit our warehouse Lefty to a tee."

"But if Michelle didn't know he was here..."

Alicia grunted, her mouth full of sandwich. She swallowed and said, "When the people in Rattlesnake Canyon told her about an encampment run by a guy named Lefty, I wonder how that hit her."

"And if Lefty dumped her and ran away to Santa Barbara, I wonder how he felt when she wandered into his camp in the middle of the night."

****

The meeting with the adoption attorney was both momentous and mundane. It turned out that as an adult, Ben didn't need permission from either of his birth parents to be adopted by me, but, ironically, I needed the permission of my spouse. Once Alicia assured the attorney of her agreement on the matter, the rest was paperwork that the attorney would prepare, have us sign, and then submit to the courts. Once that was done, the courts would contact us regarding a hearing date, and with that, Ben would legally be my child.

We celebrated with ice cream cones from McConnell's on State Street, the most touristy of the tourist thoroughfares in Santa Barbara. It's also one of the more popular places for homeless people to wander during the day. I watched Alicia eye each one who passed, barely remembering to lick her ice cream until it melted onto her fingers. I wanted to squeeze her hand and reassure her that everything was going to be okay, but I wasn't convinced of that myself.

Ben devoured the last of his Rocky Road. He licked his fingers and said, "I've been thinking about that Lefty guy. If he's ex-military, maybe the VA would have something on him, like if he got services through them or something."

I bumped Ben with my shoulder. "Great idea. If officialdom won't answer, maybe some of the guys who hang around the VA might."

"Knowing you two," Ben said, "you'll want to head right over. As much as I'd like to be part of the search party, I've got a class tonight, so could you drop me off first?"

We complied with Ben's request then took a short hop on the 101 freeway to the Calle Real offramp that led to the Santa Barbara VA Health Clinic. The nearest full-service Vet Center was in Ventura, but that was an hour bus ride away. We figured Lefty might spend more time at a local spot.

A plush, green lawn edged with tall bushes surrounded the two-story, rose-colored-brick building that housed the VA clinic. Two palm trees stood guard near the front door. Several men and a few women lounged on the lawn. Suspicious looks met us as we started toward the building.

Before we reached the entrance, the elusive animal rights activist, Sophia Carlotti, opened the door and limped out to the landing. I'm not sure which of us was more surprised.

"I've been trying to reach you," I said to Carlotti then introduced her to Alicia. "Were you leaving? Maybe we could get a cup of coffee?"

Carlotti hesitated then shrugged. "Why not? There's a decent café about five minutes down the road from here. I'll meet you there."

On the drive to the coffee shop, I apologized to Alicia for the delay in our plan. I also told her I doubted Carlotti would actually meet us at the rendezvous, but Carlotti surprised me and showed up about two minutes after we arrived.

"What do you want?" Carlotti asked as she added sugar to her cup of coffee.

Alicia jumped in before I had a chance. "Do you know a Marine Corps vet named Lefty?" She briefly explained his connection to Michelle.

Carlotti took several sips of coffee before she answered. "I know Lefty. Trained under him. He comes in and out of town. I haven't seen him in over a year. If he's back in Santa Barbara, he'll show up at the VA sooner or later."

"Do you know his real name?"

Carlotti glared at Alicia. "If he wanted you to know that, he would have told you." She started to stand. "If that's it, I need to get going."

"Not even close," I said, gesturing to her chair. "You lied to me about your connection with Highland Medical."

Carlotti's body hovered for a moment above the chair

before she eased back down. "In what way?"

"Dr. Ingrid Olsson was a member of Animals First. Dr. Nathan Sloan left part of his estate to Animals First. You're the founding mother of Animals First. So, don't give me any crap about not knowing those two."

"Sloan left us money?" Carlotti frowned down at her coffee.

I counted to ten waiting for Carlotti to continue. When she didn't, I prodded her. "You can tell me about it now or you can tell the police after I phone them and share my bits of information."

"What difference does it make to you?"

"Michelle was working at Highland on the night of the murder. She's since disappeared, and it seems at least one not-nice person is searching for her. My theory is that her being missing involves Highland Medical. And you're my link."

"If you think I somehow know where your sister-in-law is, then you're sunk. I've never met her. I know nothing about her." She shrugged. "If it helps at all, if Lefty has her back, she's in good hands. He's sharp and he's a survivor."

"As nice as that is to know, you once again totally avoided your involvement with Highland. What's going on there?"

Carlotti stared off into the distance for a full minute before she responded. When she spoke, it was as if she were addressing her remarks to the wall. "There are twenty-six million animals used to test products and drugs every year in the United States alone. Twenty-six million." She let the figure hang in the air. "And they all die either in the testing or afterward when they're butchered to see what those poisons did to their bodies. It makes me want to bomb every research facility in the country."

Carlotti picked up her coffee, only to slam the cup down on the table without taking a sip. "Jeff and I were trying to stop this insanity. He thought working with people inside the medical profession was the best way to change the system. I thought he was being a friggin' Tinkerbell with that idea, but he was determined. He made contact with Sloan. The two of them were starting to work on a more humane way to treat the test animals as well as a method to steer science away from using animals for testing, period. Jeff was good that way. Patient. Understanding."

Alicia spoke up. "Doesn't sound like the type of guy to shoot paintballs at the mayor."

Carlotti shrugged again. "I guess even saints have their limits."

I asked, "Did Jeffrey ever mention anything about irregularities in the orders for animals coming through Highland?"

Carlotti's eyes snapped to mine. "What kind of irregularities?"

"Unusual animals ordered. Or shipments of animals or equipment that were expected but never arrived."

"You're thinking smuggling or money laundering. Maybe endangered animals or animal parts. Those bastards." She gripped the end of the table so hard I expected to see dents in the wood. "I'm going to rip out Hench's throat."

"It's a theory, not a fact. You may want to wait for confirmation before cutting off Hench's air supply."

Anger radiated from Carlotti like heat from a forest fire. "You want confirmation? I'll wring a confession out of that asshole."

Chapter Nineteen

Alicia and I returned to the veteran's clinic before it closed only to be told they wouldn't release any information about anyone to us. None of the vets lounging around the center admitted to knowing Lefty or anyone matching our description of him. Alicia chewed on her lip as we sat on the grass of the center considering our next move.

Everything seemed to twirl around Highland Medical, but I was damned if I could figure out why. Too many conflicting interests and not enough information. I itched for my legal pad and computer. Writing it all down in logical groupings always helped me figure out complex cases. I needed to apply that logic to this puzzle.

Before I could suggest a return to home, Alicia's phone rang. It was Ben. She put it on speaker, and I heard a quiver in Ben's voice.

"Zach is at my school. He's standing in front of my class-room. Break time's over, but I can't go back in without him seeing me."

"Can he see you now?" I asked.

"I don't think so. I'm behind a pillar in the quad. I spotted him, but I don't think he saw me."

Alicia said, "Stay where you are. We'll be there in fifteen minutes."

Ben's voice firmed up. "No. This is something I have to handle. I'm sorry I called you." He disconnected.

Alicia's eyes narrowed as she pulled herself up from the ground. "The only one who's going to be sorry is Zacharias Wise."

****

We heard them before we saw them. As we raced across the grassy quad, the quarrelsome voices grew louder. Twenty people crowded around the pair. A couple held their phones up, recording the encounter.

Seen together, there was no denying Zach's and Ben's relationship. Both stood nearly six feet tall, and although Zach boasted the filled-out shape of a grown man, the two men had legs and muscular arms of the same length and shape. A key difference was that Zach's right arm was cocked as if ready to deliver a blow.

"Go ahead," Ben said in a loud, defiant voice. "It won't be the first time you've hit me."

"Zach, don't you dare." The steel in Alicia's voice echoed across the quad. She broke through the mob and strode up to the men like a warrior princess.

Zach ignored her, focusing his ire on Ben. "If I ever really hit you, you'd still have the scars."

"Now there's a mark of manhood." Ben sounded disgusted. "I wish I could get rid of your DNA as well as your claims to being my father."

Alicia wedged herself between them. "Stop this pissing contest right now." She stared at Zach until he dropped his fist, then she turned her gaze to Ben who took a step back. She jerked her head at the bystanders. "Let's take this discussion somewhere less public."

The dozen or so onlookers left at the cessation of hostilities. Most of the classes must have taken the same break, because the flow of students across the grassy field dropped to a dribble. I followed the trio to a deserted corner of the quad where a round, cement table and benches sat.

No one took advantage of the bench. Alicia propped her hip against the table and folded her arms. "All right, Zach, you're angry. We get that. You think beating up Ben is a good way to get him to change his mind? You haven't been drinking again, have you?"

"I haven't taken a drink in twenty years. Haven't needed one since getting rid of you."

Ben leaped forward as if to defend his mother, but Alicia raised a hand to stop him.

"You have a new wife and three kids. Why worry about what Ben does or doesn't do?"

"He's my first-born son."

"So?" Alicia shook her head. "Please tell me you're not stuck on that primogeniture crap."

"It's not crap and you know it. My first-born son is my primary heir. You may have turned your back on our religion, but I hold it sacred."

Ben stepped forward. "I have no idea what you're talking about, but I'll make it easy for you. Disinherit me. I'm not your son in any real way. You were a sperm donor. That's all." He waved his arm in my direction. "Kate was there when I was born, and she's been with me ever since. I love her as much as I love Mom. I don't know much about you, and what I do know, I don't like. So, feel free to consider the son in your new family as your first-born. That would be a relief for me." He snatched his backpack. "I'm late to class."

The three of us watched Ben's back as he stomped across the grass toward the classrooms.

Zach turned to me, his jaw clenched. "You took my wife, now you've taken my son. Punishment is coming to you." His voice broke. He pivoted and marched stiffly down the pathway to the parking lot.

"I hope he meant that in the Biblical sense."

Alicia hugged me. "I wouldn't count on it."

✳✳✳✳

The ride home was silent. We agreed to take a break from all serious discussion as we rummaged through the refrigerator and pantry for a wild assortment of left-over meat, cheeses, fruit, and crackers to call dinner. We settled in the living room, feet on the coffee table, and watched the waves undulating on the ocean in an attempt to soothe our overheated brains. I don't think it worked for either of us.

I tried to abide by our agreement, but I needed to understand one point. "So, what is this 'primo genesis' thing that Zach pitched a fit about?"

"Primogeniture. In more conservative Jewish practices, the first-born son is the primary beneficiary of a father's will. He's supposed to get double what any others get. Of course, there's no similar provision for girls. Sexist and stupid. It goes back to when they didn't want to have property divided

up into smaller and smaller pieces over succeeding genera-
tions."

"Zach believes in this?"

Alicia shrugged. "He never mentioned it to me before. But he grew up in a rather conservative sect of Judaism. More towards the orthodox side of thinking than the reform."

"How did a liberal, radical like you go over with his family?"

"Not well. His father tried to forbid the marriage. Zach was young and rebellious and refused to listen to him." Alicia sat up and hunched forward. "I guess he's reverting more and more to the way he was brought up."

I nibbled on an apple slice topped with Swiss cheese while contemplating the complexities of Zach. "He's been sort of a lost and damaged soul for a long time. God knows what the Gulf War did to him. Maybe he needs firm ground under his feet. Tradition can give that feeling to you."

Alicia turned and raised an eyebrow at me. "You're certainly in a forgiving mood for a woman who's been threatened with Godly vengeance."

"Zach's prayers will have to get in line. You should have heard some of the threats of divine intervention I received from losing litigants."

"Divine intervention is exactly what we need in Michelle's case. Maybe I should be lighting more candles instead of running after questionable bits of information."

I kissed her on the forehead. "Put some of those candles around the tub and have a nice soak. Council duty calls. I have to go to the Community Policing ad hoc committee meeting. Maybe somebody there will be from the Restorative Policing Unit with some ideas about Michelle that we haven't thought of." I squeezed her shoulders. "See you between the sheets."

****

Over breakfast, I told a still sleepy Alicia the police unit working with the homeless weren't in attendance at last night's meeting, but the sergeant at the meeting gave me some ideas about finding Michelle. "She suggested we have

Keesha check both the post office and the twenty-four-hour laundromat at the crack of dawn one day. Some homeless people are always taking shelter there. The other place to check out is a camp under the freeway near Goleta. It's got several inhabitants who've been in the area for years. If Lefty is a fixture around these parts, they might know him."

Alicia managed a grunt of assent. I knew she didn't sleep well last night. She was tossing around on the bed when I came home, and her side was cold and empty when I got up at seven. I poured her more coffee, but even caffeine didn't activate her vocal cords.

"I have to go to the City Council chambers this morning. The subcommittee on Homelessness and Community Relations is meeting, and I want to see if I can talk to a few of the experts they're interviewing. Then I have the council meeting this afternoon. Do you want me to call Keesha before I leave, or do you want to?"

Alicia pointed a finger at me and tottered off toward the shower, coffee mug clenched in her fist.

My call to Collins caught her as she was driving. I relayed the police officer's suggestions, and she assured me she already hit those locations.

"I found out a couple of things. One, Lefty's name is Alexander Garland. Sergeant Garland of the U.S. Marine Corps, to be exact. Served in Afghanistan and Iraq. Suffering from a variety of PTSD symptoms. Homeless since two months after being released from the service."

"Poor guy. Another vet we haven't helped."

"The other thing. A tentative sighting of Michelle in an encampment on the outskirts of town. I'm heading there now."

"What? Where?" I snapped up my keys. "We'll meet you there."

"Not a good idea. Let me check it out. If I can confirm anything, I'll notify you then. Right now, you've got a nervous filly who may bolt if we send in a platoon. It's a one-person reconnaissance job."

I wanted to argue but saw the wisdom of her position, despite her mixed cowpoke and military metaphors. "All right. But call or text any time. Don't worry about interrupting a meeting or anything."

"As soon as I know anything concrete, I'll let you know. I'll come by in the late afternoon, and we can touch base. Remember to breathe in the meantime."

****

Deep breaths didn't help when I ran into the dear mayor on my way to the council chambers.

"Stay out of the Highland Medical expansion project." Thompson waved her finger in my direction. "This is one business deal that you shouldn't mess with. It's going to bring massive revenue to the city, so quit poking your nose into it."

"Massive revenues to the city, or to your re-election campaign?"

The mayor's face reddened. "Are you accusing me of something?"

"I'm wondering how the expansion of a major donor to your campaign is going to help the city. I haven't seen numbers showing Highland as much of a generator of income for the city. Shareholders maybe, but not Santa Barbara."

Thompson stepped closer and lowered her voice. "These guys are on the verge of a very important medical breakthrough. When it comes, they'll hold the royalties and the demand for the drug is going to go through the roof. We get a huge boost from property taxes now, and they'll be hiring over a hundred new employees just to meet the demand when the product breaks."

"If the product breaks. If it makes it through trials. If, if, if. And what property tax increase will we see? When they built the lab, the city waived taxes for the first five years and promised below-rate taxes for the next five."

Thompson's eyes narrowed. "You really don't understand business and investment. You think short-term, not long-term, and the city can't survive that way."

"The city also can't survive by depending on a polluting or unethical company." I spun around and headed for the council chambers. I knew I let her get to me, but I wasn't sure why. Usually, I can brush aside the slings and arrows flung my way by opponents, but Thompson was a different matter.

Muttering to myself, I made my way to the back row of the chambers where the meeting had already begun. A second later I was joined by John Johnson.

The reporter gave no greeting but merely leaned toward me and whispered, "My police sources tell me your sister-in-law is now a person of interest in the Highland murder."

Chapter Twenty

I skipped the meeting and rushed home. True to Johnson's prediction, a duo of police detectives occupied my living room when I returned. I don't know what went on before I got there, but Alicia was giving them an icy stare that didn't bode well for the conversation.

"Ma'am, we need to speak with your sister."

"And I'll tell you once again, I don't know where she is."

"You're sure she has no friends in the area?"

I answered the question as I entered the room. "Michelle has us. She has her niece and nephew. None of us have seen her since we reported her missing. We even checked in with the police when that unidentified body was found by the hiking trail to make sure it wasn't Michelle." I sat on the arm of the chair where Alicia settled and introduced myself. "Have you checked all the homeless encampments?"

"We're making inquiries."

"Why now? What's changed since the day of Sloan's death?"

The detective tapped his pen against his notebook before replying, "Witnesses have come forward who saw Michelle Mazer leaving Highland Medical the evening of the murder. With a gun."

****

"Damn, Damn. Damn." Alicia punctuated each proclamation with a slap on the kitchen counter. "What has Michelle gotten herself into this time?"

"Keesha hasn't called yet?"

"No. Which means Michelle wasn't there."

"Possibly." My lawyerly mind held an aversion to absolutes. "But Keesha promised to come around this afternoon, so we'll know for sure then. Switching streams, Zach keeps creeping into my mind. Did you talk with Ben today?"

Alicia shook her head. "I meant to, but by the time I was ready to face the world, the police were knocking on the door." She found her phone and punched the button for Ben on speed dial.

"At work. Can't talk," Ben said. In a quick reversal, he added, "The police are back questioning everybody. I heard them talking about a blocked security camera and something about the cleaning crew. But no one's mentioned Aunt Michelle by name." Murmuring came over the line before we heard Ben say, "Oops. Gotta go."

Alicia said, "I guess that means Ben isn't being hassled by Zach at the moment. That's one bit of good news." She sighed and slumped in her chair. "I'm not normally a pessimist, but I've got to admit, I don't see how any of this can turn out well for Michelle."

****

My unexpected trip home meant I ran late for the council meeting. In my absence, protestors with picket signs had gathered in front of city hall. Animal activists chanted indecipherable slogans while anti-development protestors encouraged drivers to honk their horns in support. The resulting cacophony was not a good omen for a peaceful council meeting.

I waded my way through the concerned citizens who filled the overflow balcony of the chambers then squeezed through the packed chambers up to the raised dais. Three uniformed, armed officers stood on guard in front of the stage. They waved me through. I managed to reach my seat right as the flag salute ended. My late entry earned a glare from the mayor.

I scanned the crowd and saw that Red Boyle managed to attend despite her injury. I also noticed several people wearing Animals First shirts, but Carlotti was not among them. In fact, the spokesperson for Animals First looked ill at ease as she read a prepared speech. Her delivery evidenced none of the passion or persuasiveness that Carlotti exhibited. I wondered why Carlotti wasn't in attendance.

True to her word, Boyle headed up a number of speakers from MEAP heaping scorn on the council for even considering the expansion of Highland Medical. With each speaker, Thompson's face grew redder and her eyes progressively narrowed. Luckily, the public comment time ran out before the mayor experienced a stroke on stage.

My motion to study the nonlethal ways of dealing with the ground squirrel menace passed without debate. When the subject of the mayor's plan to corral and ship off the homeless was introduced for debate, Reynaldo Sanchez jumped in.

"I ask that the council direct staff to study a proposal that Councilmember Matthews submitted regarding the use of excess municipal and commercial property in the city as both shelters and services centers for the homeless."

Thompson ignored him. "The motion before the council provides for the humane housing of the homeless while also protecting public safety."

Boos erupted from the audience. I wasn't surprised to find that a sizeable number of homeless activists managed to attend the meeting as well.

Several of the council members spoke regarding the issue. All of them mentioned my proposal as well as the mayor's. A "friendly amendment" was made to incorporate both proposals in the study. It passed with only one dissenting vote, that of the mayor.

Thompson didn't wait for the council chambers to clear after the meeting before snarling at me. "How dare you stir up trouble and bring agitators to this meeting? Sharing confidential council information is a breach of public trust and an ethics violation. I should have you brought up on charges."

Aware that most of the other council members, along with some of the crowd, were an audience to our discussion, I tried to keep it civil. "If you're talking about the proposed expansion of Highland Medical, the general public seemed to know about it before I did."

"Oh, sure. It's merely a coincidence that you're working to block this and a bunch of loonies with signs happened to show up when it wasn't even on the agenda."

A murmur of disapproval swept the crowd. I spotted Johnson on the edge of the crowd and groaned silently. I imagined how the "loonies" comment was going to play in the newspaper and who the mayor would blame for it. "Look, Julia, I didn't leak any council information to the public. I didn't invite protestors to the meeting. And I've got far more important things going on in my life than planning ways to embarrass you in front of the world. Besides, you seem to be doing a swell job of that all by yourself."

****

I couldn't shake the feeling that Carlotti's absence at the council meeting was a bad sign. Considering her homicidal threats when we last met, I wondered if I should have warned Kyle Hench and associates to be on the lookout for her. My suspicion that she knew more than she was sharing made me uneasy as well. Since I knew Alicia would be out late on a real estate appointment, I decided to ease my mind and make a short stop on the way home. I bounded up the steps to the offices of Animals First. The CLOSED sign hung in the window of the door, but I pounded on it anyway. The door swung open on its own accord.

Having been attacked once before in a supposedly safe space, I glanced around the outer hallway for a defensive weapon. Spying a broken broomstick handle that was leaned against a trashcan, I grabbed it and used it to push the door further open.

The creak of the hinge did nothing to soothe my nerves. Steeling myself, I swung the door fully open.

File folders were strewn over the floor and desk. The bottom file cabinet drawers hung open. I listened for any noises, any signs of another person in the room. Nothing. I stepped silently into the office and saw that the desk drawers were pulled out and tossed into a corner of the room. Papers covered the floor.

I stepped around the desk. The desk chair was overturned, its seat shredded.

Even the photos on the walls were crooked on their hangers, as if someone was looking for a hidden safe. I went over to the one that showed the mountain lion and its rescuers, including Olsson, the absent Highland Medical researcher. I thought of Carlotti's odd reaction to my touching that photo. I took two tissues from my pocket and covered my fingers. I removed the ten-by-twelve-inch picture frame. I turned it over and ran my fingers along the backing. I felt a slight lump. I took out my two-inch Swiss Army knife, sliced open the back, and slid out three sheets of letter-sized paper.

I saw the Highland Medical Research and Development letterhead on one. A war with my conscience ensued. I wanted time to examine the papers, but taking them with me was theft, a clear violation of the law and my oath as an officer of the courts. Then, I spotted a copier in the corner of the room. It hadn't been vandalized, so I quickly fed the pages through. I put the copies into my pocket, slid the originals back behind the picture, rehung the photo, and called the police.

While I waited for their arrival, I opened the pages. The first one contained scientific jargon and made little sense to me. I didn't have time to read the others. Sirens neared. I hastily folded the copies and returned them to my pocket.

The police were not impressed with my rationale for entering the office. I was questioned by both the officers who arrived on the scene and then, thirty minutes later, by the detectives in charge of burglary. Since the police were unable to reach Carlotti by phone or in person either, they finally let me leave with the understanding I would show up at the police station the next day to give a full report.

I sped back to my home office and unfolded the once-hidden notes. I felt a momentary pang about copying these papers without permission. The lawyer in me shuddered. I promised myself that I would destroy them once I reviewed them to see if they offered any lead to the mess at Highland and, in turn, to Michelle.

Putting aside the one sheet I'd skimmed at Carlotti's office, I read through the other two. The first held a list from a political action committee. The Moving Forward PAC was not one I'd heard of, but the recipients of its money involved many familiar names. The list included three members of the planning commission, two council members, and the mayor. The amounts were double what I'd spent on my modest campaign for my council seat and well over the legal limit for a direct contribution to a candidate by a PAC. Of course, a political action committee could give unlimited funds in indirect support of a campaign. That may be the meaning of the totals. Maybe not. I foresaw siccing Lily onto this list.

The second page displayed the logo for Highland Medical. It seemed to be a purchase order from Highland to a Class A animal supplier for dogs, cats, rabbits, and rats. There were two types of dealers for test animals. Class A were breeders of animals specifically for lab use while Class B sold animals from wherever they could find them including animal shelters, lost pets, and unsold pet store stock. My gut reaction to both sources was a silent scream.

Finally, I tackled the scientific paper. It made no more sense to me now than when I was at Carlotti's place. I began looking up what seemed like every other word. It contained a lot of chemicals that were components of current prescription drugs, but not in the combinations listed on the paper. Some of the compounds looked to be used mainly in animals. And I couldn't find information on one of them at all.

Ben. Of course. Why was I trying to dust off my high school chemistry knowledge, when an expert witness was on hand? I texted Ben and asked him to call me or come by the house when he got out of work. I scanned the page and printed out a copy for Ben. Then I placed all three papers in my office safe.

Next, I printed out a map of Santa Barbara and put dots on every place we'd checked for Michelle. Grey dots for the ones with no leads, blue for possible sightings, and red for the hot ones where we knew she'd been. I put in yellow dots for areas suggested by others where homeless people gathered or slept, but that we hadn't visited yet. I incorporated all the places Alicia and Collins searched as well.

No pattern to the colors emerged.

I decided to add a time and date to the red ones to see if I could figure any rhyme or reason to Michelle's wanderings. I noticed that, other than the camp at Rattlesnake Canyon, she hadn't been seen at any of the other encampments near Highland Medical. Was it deliberate or was she merely trying to reach Lefty?

I heard the backdoor open and Ben's voice calling out.

After greetings and his reassurances that the police hadn't been interested in him, personally, I showed him the paper without explaining where I found it. "I need your expertise to decipher it."

Ben frowned over the words, occasionally tapping into his phone before grunting and skimming downward again over the paper with his finger. "This seems to be a drug interaction list of some sort. These on the left are similar to drugs used in chemotherapy and in immunotherapy. On the right are various solutions. The notes on the bottom reflect the results of combining one or more of these drug compounds."

"Is there anything in there that's proprietary or cutting edge or totally unusual or possibly valuable in any way?"

Ben shook his head. "The combinations are unusual, but without the amounts of each of the chemicals going into the compounds, I can't tell you there's anything in here that's a breakthrough drug. Of course, there could be something like that and I just don't recognize it."

"Then why would someone go through a great deal of trouble to hide it?"

"This was hidden? Shit, Ma. Tell me you aren't breaking and entering or some other nasty thing that's going to get you thrown in jail again."

"Tales of my time in jail are wildly exaggerated." I pointed to the paper. "Know anyone else who might be able to give us a more in-depth analysis of what's on that page?"

"A few. Let me borrow this, and I'll let you know what I find out."

"Ben, please be careful who you show it to. Make it people you know and trust."

"Discretion is my middle name. At least it might be." Ben chuckled. "Once you adopt me, I'm planning on making a few changes."

****

Collins and Alicia arrived at the house within minutes of each other. After declining a beverage, Collins flipped out her notebook computer and clicked open a file. Alicia and I crowded next to her as she showed photos of an assortment of tents and cardboard boxes arrayed under a freeway bridge. She pointed to a green-and-grey-nylon tent.

"That's where Michelle was staying up until two days ago. She and Alexander Garland AKA Lefty. She's known as Shelly, and she and Lefty are pretty popular with most of the other residents. But one guy was not a fan, and he gave me most of the information."

"Are you sure? Two days ago? Sunday?" Alicia burst into tears and buried her head in my shoulder.

I glanced at Collins who looked down at her computer screen. Unsure what was going on, I held Alicia until the storm seemed to pass. I handed her a tissue.

As she wiped her eyes, she explained, "Michelle was alive two days ago. That means she can't be the dead woman they found. I've been so worried." She teared up again.

Collins kept her head down. It seemed she was allowing Alicia the time she needed to gather herself. When all was quiet again, she looked up and reported that Michelle and Lefty arrived at the camp Saturday. They set up their tent and stayed close to the bridge day and night. Lefty went off on Sunday and returned with several sacks of food, which he shared with others in the area. The informant didn't get what he considered his fair share, thus the disgruntlement.

Michelle and Lefty disappeared when a man came to the camp Sunday afternoon asking questions. The guy said he was a census worker, but the people in the camp didn't believe him and wouldn't talk with him. The man gave up and left, but Michelle and Lefty didn't return, not even to collect their tent, which was now being claimed by the informant.

Collins concluded, "Not much of a description of the guy. Average height and build. Baseball hat and sunglasses, so no one was sure about hair or eye color. No facial hair or tats."

"They were there on Sunday. So close," Alicia said with a sigh.

"There's more news," Collins said, paging to a map of Santa Barbara. "Two of the people in the freeway camp admitted they knew Lefty and gave me some of his favorite places to sleep. I covered most of them this morning and will check the others tonight when people tend to settle into their homes for the evening." She pointed out all the spots.

"You might want to concentrate on the ones that are farthest from Highland Medical," I said. I took out the map I'd constructed earlier and pointed to the dots. "See, all the red and blue ones are far from the medical center. There are several closer to the building, but there haven't been any signs of Michelle staying there."

Collins studied the map and compared it to the one on her computer. She took a photo of it with her phone. "Could be a coincidence, but I'll start with the distant ones tonight."

"I should go with you," Alicia said. "Maybe people will talk to me when they know I'm her sister."

I held back a comment on the lack of effectiveness of that approach so far. I was glad when Collins declined her offer.

Collins said, "First of all, these are not the best areas and I don't want to try to keep both of us safe at the same time. And I haven't seen personal approaches work as much as a little monetary incentive. When you get my bill, you'll see how much it can take to get people to talk."

****

The next morning, I ducked into my City Council office and gathered all the notices of upcoming motions, resolutions, and staff recommendations. My intention was to shove them into a folder then dash off to give my statement to the police about the break-in at the Animals First office. However, the blinking light on my office phone caught my eye. It showed three messages. I considered ignoring it, but guilt over not giving my job the attention it deserved drove me to click the Message button.

The first call was from a constituent regarding a pothole in one of the residential streets. I forwarded it to the city manager so that he could schedule a repair crew.

The second call was from the reporter, Johnson. "I trust my tip about your sister-in-law helped you out. Now, maybe, you can help me. I'd like to talk with you about your friend, the mayor, and some of her financial dealings. Give me a call."

I deleted the message. Whatever witch hunt Johnson was

on, I wanted no part of it. I had my own problems.

The third call was not one I expected. Highland Medical's chief researcher, Dr. Kyle Hench's voice sounded over the line. He requested a meeting at my convenience.

I checked the time and date of the message. Yesterday, about an hour after my first run-in with the mayor. I wonder how many of my slurs on the company's reputation Thompson conveyed to him. No doubt, all of them.

I toyed with the idea of making Hench come to me. I thought I might get more out of him if he wasn't on his home turf. But Highland is where Michelle disappeared. I couldn't shake the feeling that being there might give me more of a clue about why she ran and where.

I ended up calling and setting up an appointment for later in the morning at his office, figuring my statement to the police might take an hour. I immediately placed another call, this time to my trusty ex-paralegal, Lily.

"Hey, boss. I was going to call you today. But I've been swamped by the people who pay my salary. I was able to find some information on your Dr. Olsson, but I haven't found out where she is yet."

"You're the best. Could you email me what you have? I also have a page regarding a political action committee that I'll fax you. I'd like to know about the committee, its donors, and the recipients of its money."

"I see," Lily said. "This list wouldn't include any of your political enemies, would it?"

"You know me. I don't have enemies, only people who haven't figured out I'm a friend. Besides all that, I have a question about some of the material you sent me on Highland Medical. The file said that Highland was owned by two other companies, but you couldn't find any shareholders or Board of Directors. Did Dr. Kyle Hench's name come up in any of your research?"

The click of computer keys sounded over the line. "Yeah. He's listed as the chief operating officer of Highland Medical, but I don't know if he has any connection to either of the parent companies because I still can't find board listings for them. They're privately held companies, so the SEC has no public information on them."

"Have there been any complaints against Highland or either of the parent companies for any kind of misconduct?"

"Can you be a little more specific, boss? That covers everything from fraud to sexual harassment to employee complaints about the break room. Is there anything in particular you want me to check out?"

"Environmental issues or animal abuse. Maybe even ties to drug cartels or money laundering."

Lily hissed. "Bad guys. Got it."

"One other thing. Would you check out a reporter for the *Santa Barbara News Press*? His name is John Johnson, Jr."

"Has he been writing nasty things about you?"

"No. He's just popping up a bit too often for my taste."

"Okay, boss. Call you within a few days. And I'll email you about Dr. Olsson when we hang up."

Lily was true to her word, and within a minute I was printing out three pages on the life and times of Dr. Ingrid Olsson.

Despite her very Scandinavian name, Olsson was born and raised in the Midwest. She was an only child. Her father was a teacher, and her mother a gynecologist. Both were deceased. She earned her bachelor's degree in Massachusetts but moved to California for her doctoral studies. Olsson earned both an MD and a PhD through the Medical Scientist Training Program at UCLA.

During her eight years of medical school, she met and married a fellow med student, Joseph Henderson. It didn't appear that she changed her name to his as her diploma was awarded to Ingrid Olsson.

Her work history was short. Before Highland Medical, she worked for UCLA and USC as a research scientist. Her exact field of study seemed to be classified as Lily made no note of it.

The last page showed a copy of a birth certificate for the child of Ingrid and Joseph, along with Joseph's death certificate. The cause of death for Joseph at the young age of thirty-two was cancer. The birth certificate was for a son, Jeffrey Henderson.

Chapter Twenty-One

Jeffrey Henderson. The paint-ball-shooting animal rights activist, murder victim was Dr. Ingrid Olsson's son.

I stared at the name for several seconds. Eventually, it occurred to me why Olsson looked familiar to me when I met her. She had passed along her angular facial bone structure and the shape of her eyes to her son.

Now Dr. Olsson's involvement with Animals First took on a new layer of meaning. Her son was its chief recruiter. Did he draw her into animal activism, or did he inherit that tendency from her?

Given that she trained in a field that depended heavily on animal testing, my bet lay with him as the consciousness raiser. But how invested in animal rights was she? After all, she still worked in a testing facility.

Or was she a mole for Animals First?

With Jeffrey dead and the good doctor missing, I wasn't sure I would ever find out the truth of that relationship. But it got me thinking that Animals First was somehow entwined in this whole quagmire around Michelle. I just didn't know how.

I glanced out the window at the parking lot. A truck towing a powerboat pulled in. The boat was filled with fishing equipment, no doubt back from a morning on the ocean. The poles and tackle boxes made me think that I didn't have enough useful tidbits to bait a hook to catch the fish I was after, so I was going to have to go with a net. I dashed off another email to Lily adding to her workload. I asked for any information she could uncover on Animals First and Sophia Carlotti, as well as Dr. Kyle Hench. Then I widened the net even more and added Mayor Thompson to the list.

I looked again at the twenty-foot fishing boat in the lot. I wondered if a net was going to be enough or if, like in *Jaws,* I'd need a bigger boat.

****

Kyle Hench's mouth curved upward when I was escorted into his office, but the expression seemed tight.

I relaxed into a plush chair and placed the ball firmly in his court. "What can I do for you, Doctor?"

"I understand you have some concerns regarding Highland Medical." He listed the items I'd flung at the mayor. At the end of the litany, he spread his hands wide. "I thought I addressed those issues, but it appears I was mistaken."

"You gave me answers but no verification. It's as if you made claims about your drugs but didn't have proof of their efficacy. I doubt they'd go on to clinic trials."

Hench stiffened and raised an eyebrow. "I'm not clear what you're talking about."

"I was trying to give you an example you might understand. As a scientist, you need to show verifiable proof. As a council member, I need proof to show my constituents that Highland is an ethical company that doesn't abuse animals and doesn't pollute the environment."

"Ah." He gave a genial smile. "Of course. I see. Environmental and safety concerns. Our public relations department has all our statistics and governmental inspection reports. I'll ask them to send a copy to you." He stood.

I raised a finger. "One more matter."

Hench sank back into his chair.

"Are you developing new drugs, or are you combining existing ones in new ways?"

"We do both."

"Does the company make more money one way or the other?"

"That depends. As I think I told you before, getting a new drug approved takes years of research, development, and safety testing. But if a drug is already approved to treat one condition or disease, and we can find another purpose for it, that saves a great deal of time and money. The trick to that is knowing what existing drugs to consider for the treatment of the disease you're working on."

"Does that apply to finding that a combination of

approved drugs works to benefit something other than what they are approved for?"

"New drug therapies can take myriad forms. It can be one drug used in a different way or a combination of two or more drugs to treat a different disease." He halted his lecture, frowning. "But what does any of this have to do with the concerns of your constituents?"

Good question, I thought. I scrambled a bit. "If you're using known drugs, then the safe ways to handle and dispose of them must be well documented. That will ease the anxiety of those who fear toxic dump sites invading the city. And I'm sure that animal testing on those drugs is minimal since the Federal Drug Administration has already deemed them safe. If true, that would make the animal rights people happier." I smiled to demonstrate that I wasn't one of those naïve people. I couldn't tell if Hench bought it, but he relaxed and smiled in return.

"I understand. Science scares a lot of people, especially with all the crazies out there who think we're the scourge of the earth, determined to destroy mankind."

I didn't tell him I could sympathize with that point of view.

✻✻✻✻

Sarah was dancing Amy around the backyard when I arrived home. Their giggles lifted my spirits like few things in this world could. I cut in, claiming Amy as a dance partner, and blew air against her tummy causing even more peals of laughter.

I cradled her in my arms and regarded her mother. "To what do I owe this delightful interlude? Need some unexpected babysitting?"

"No. My class was cancelled, and with the police interested in my caseload, HR asked me to take a few days leave until the whole mess is resolved."

"So why bring my delightful granddaughter here? Is David trying to concentrate at home?"

Sarah waved her arm toward the vista of ocean and Channel Islands that was our backyard. "The view is better here."

"You two could buy a place along the coast. You can afford it." David had unexpectedly inherited a substantial fortune in the last year.

She shook her head. "You know David won't touch that money. If we use it at all, it will go to environmental projects. We're living on what we earn."

"In that case, you'll be visiting our backyard for a very long time. And I love it." I put Amy in her playpen, and Sarah and I settled in two lounge chairs. I filled Sarah in on most of what happened with Michelle and with Zach and Ben's confrontation.

Sarah asked the same question I had. "What the hell is primogeniture?"

As I explained the concept to her, I watched astonishment flood her face.

"You have got to be kidding me. That doesn't sound like the Dad I know. What world is he living in?"

"A safe one for him. Traditions can give people security when the world's a little crazy."

Her incredulous stare transferred its target to me. "You're supporting a patriarchal, not to mention Neanderthal, approach to inheritance rights?"

I held up my hands in surrender. "Don't shoot the messenger. I can understand Zach's point of view without agreeing with it. I know that's not fashionable, but as you should know from law school, it's a skill that works well in court cases."

"Court is one thing. Real life is quite another. And my brother is real life, not an abstract argument." She turned and frowned at the ocean. "I'm so blown away by this. I don't even know what I'll say to Dad the next time I talk to him."

I toyed with suggesting that she not talk to him but thought better of it.

An excited squeal from Amy distracted both of us. An ant was crawling over her arm. She giggled and waved her fists. Sarah spoiled the fun by whisking the ant away before rejoining me.

"I meant to tell you," she said. "I think Animals First was the group behind the appointment that Jeffrey Henderson made. Or someone made for him. Whatever. In any case, one of their members tried to call me at the law firm."

"Did you find out why they wanted to see you?"

"Not exactly. They left a message yesterday about wanting legal advice about the purchase of animals for research. I tried to call back, but no one answered. So, I left a message in return telling them I'd be out of the office for a while and that if it was urgent, they should talk to our director."

"Do you remember the name?"

"Yeah. It was Sophia Carlotti."

"I wonder if that was before or after her office got ransacked." I gave Sarah an abbreviated version of the statement I gave the police earlier that morning. "The detective seemed to focus on Carlotti's political actions. I don't know who would be so against protecting animals that they would rip through her office like that."

Sarah retrieved a toy that Amy had tossed over the wall of her play area. For an infant, Amy sure exhibited a strong arm. I found my thoughts wandering as to whether they'd allow women to play professional baseball by the time she was older.

Sarah brought me back to the present by saying, "If the looters were against animal rights or some weird stuff like that, they'd spray paint slogans or trash the place. From what you describe, they weren't out to make a statement. They were looking for something. I wonder what Sophia Carlotti has that someone else wants so much?"

I thought of the papers residing in my office safe and the fact that Ben was even now showing a copy of one of them to other people. I really hoped that wasn't the buried treasure others were seeking.

Chapter Twenty-Two

Lunch consisted of a slapped-together sandwich consumed in my car on my way to an appearance at a new store opening at the Mesa Shopping Center. Store openings in my district were one of my official council duties. Smile, shake hands, wave, speak. On bad days, I felt like a well-trained dog at these events. Most times, I was glad to support our burgeoning business district. Today, despite my pressing personal woes, I felt pleased to see this particular shop opening.

The cresting ocean waves sparkled to my left before I rounded the curve on Shoreline Drive and headed inland a half mile to the two-block-long, outdoor Mesa Shopping Center that housed a large grocery store, pastry shop, restaurant, convenience store, and drug store.

I found a parking space in the tight lot, mentally adding parking to my council list of things to address, it being a key challenge for the city. Four bunches of multicolored balloons covered the windows, and a large, inflatable Husky guarded the entrance of the new Pat's Pet Rescue, a nonprofit organization. The organization owned a large piece of land in the hills above Santa Barbara where they kept most of the animals they rescued, but they wanted a storefront to bring adoptable pets to the people.

Pat Faulkner, the head of the nonprofit, welcomed me to the party with a hug. Her wide face held an abundance of wrinkles, but, rather than age, these were the kind that came from long hours in the sun and even more hours of laughing. I met Pat soon after moving to Santa Barbara when we were in search of a vet for our cat, Ginger. Pat not only connected us with a fabulous vet but also convinced us to volunteer with her group. We've been friends since that time.

The *News Press* sent a photographer and reporter to cover the opening. I was relieved that it wasn't Johnson. Pat and I cut the bright blue ribbon that fronted the door, allowing dozens of patrons to stream into the shop and ooh and ahh over the cats, dogs, birds, and amphibians available for adoption.

A plaque with major donors' names hung near the front door. I noticed that Animals First was listed. I asked Pat about their connection.

"Ever meet Sophia Carlotti?" At my nod, she said, "Sophia may be a curmudgeon when it comes to people, but she's extremely generous with anything to do with saving animals." Pat pointed to the play area where potential adopters could play with the animals. "She researched the best ways to get animals adopted and came up with the plan and the money for that. She also put us in touch with some of her major donors. With money tight, sharing donor contact info is not the norm for charities. But that's just the way Sophia is."

"Do you happen to know where she lives?"

"Yep." Pat punched the keypad on her phone and showed it to me.

For once I wouldn't need to rely on my GPS. The address was one block from where Ben and his friends lived. I knew where I was headed as soon as I could excuse myself from the grand opening party.

****

The Oak Park area of Santa Barbara has sections of older, Craftsman-style homes. A three-foot-tall, wrought iron fence wrapped around the front yard of the house where Sophia Carlotti lived. The pickets on the fence all ended in sharp points that appeared more functional than ornamental. Blooming potted flowers lined the covered front porch. Two cats lounged there in padded chairs.

When I stepped out of my car, three mismatched dogs bounded to the fence, yapping and growling. The growler was a collie mix that was missing an ear. The barker was some sort of boxer with a prosthetic left front leg. The third was a mutt with only one eye, who peered at me suspiciously but didn't make a sound.

"C'mon, girls. Heel." Carlotti appeared on the porch. She

smacked her hand against her thigh, and all three dogs hastened to her side and sat quietly. "What do you want?" Her growl was even less friendly than her dogs'.

"Help."

Carlotti thoroughly scratched the collie's head and along both flanks before waving me through the front gate. She picked up one of the cats and placed it in her lap as she took its place on the chair. I did the same with the calico that occupied the second chair.

"I'm relieved to see you're okay. I've tried to contact you several times. Did you hear from the police about your office?"

Carlotti lifted an eyebrow. "Do you want chit chat or help?"

"Okay. You said Jeffrey Henderson was working with Dr. Sloan. Was he also working with Dr. Hench or Dr. Olsson?"

"Hench wouldn't listen to anyone. No way Jeff would even have tried."

"Dr. Olsson?"

"Out of all the people working there, why are you asking about her?"

"Because she's his mother."

Carlotti didn't seem surprised by this bit of information, nor did she respond.

"Then there's the fact that Olsson helped Animals First in their rescues." It was a conjecture rather than a fact, but I wasn't about to split hairs over this. "Was she a spy for you at Highland Medical?"

"We don't need spies to know that Highland is doing unnecessary harm to animals."

"But you needed her, and you needed Sloan for something. Now one's dead and the other's missing. Combined with Jeffrey's murder, I'd think that might give you cause for concern."

"What makes you think I'm not concerned?"

Several quiet seconds passed as I stared at Carlotti, but my gaze and the silence didn't break her. Figuring a direct question was my best, and possibly last, shot, I asked, "What, exactly, is Highland doing that worries you?"

"You mean other than the money laundering or the smuggling you mentioned?" Carlotti stretched out her metal leg and rubbed her left thigh before answering. "Ingrid Olsson thought something odd was going on with the orders for testing animals. Too many orders, too many animals. But she never saw the animals shipped in, so she couldn't be sure. That was Nathan Sloan's job. So, Jeff worked his way in and got close to Sloan. Jeff told me he was on the trail of something big. He got copies of some incriminating information, but he didn't think it was enough to bring them down. He decided to try to put political pressure on the company, to see if that would help pop open the coverup. Jeff contacted the mayor and three other council members, but none of them would listen to him." Carlotti glared at me. "When he looked into the backgrounds of those wonderful public servants, he found out they were all in Highland's pocket. Big surprise. I think that's when he decided to shake you hacks up by paintballing you."

I considered reminding her that Jeffrey never contacted me, but I didn't want to stop this sudden flow of information.

Carlotti shifted her gaze to the front yard again. The collie pushed its nose against her hand, as if sensing her distress. She stroked the dog's silky nose and head before continuing. "When you said Highland was laundering money, it clicked. The big orders that weren't filled. Orders for animals that weren't needed. That meant these guys were even bigger scums than I thought. Drug money is the dirtiest business around. I saw too many guys hooked on that crap in the Marines."

"If that's what Jeffrey found out, why didn't he go to the police? Money laundering is a federal crime."

Carlotti shrugged. "Don't know. But it wouldn't have made a difference. I just got back from talking with the Feds both in Ventura and Los Angeles. No one would give me the time of day without concrete proof. Oh, they filled out forms, but you know those papers were round-filed as soon as I left the office."

"Somebody must have thought you kept proof of something or they wouldn't have searched your office quite so enthusiastically."

"Yeah, I saw it."

"Anything missing?"

Carlotti stood. "Nice of you to drop by. Don't do it again."

****

I cruised by the underpass that Keesha Collins had identified as Michelle's last place of residence. Five tents and three piles of belongings took up most of the sidewalk under the freeway. I saw a green-and-grey-nylon tent like Collins described as belonging to Michelle and Lefty. It was still set up but deserted. No one seemed to have claimed the empty dwelling. I pulled over up the road from the underpass and strode back to the tent. It was zipped closed.

Three people were huddled near what I presumed to be their belongings. I asked them all if Lefty or Shelly left anything behind when they disappeared.

"People leave stuff. Finders, keepers." A young man with long hair and a full mustache and beard peered at me as if he needed glasses to bring me into focus. "Who are you, anyway?"

I explained my relationship to Michelle and asked his name. He told me it was Tim.

"Be nice if my family would try to find me. They wish I'd never been born." Tim ran his forearm under his nose. "That disclosure is coming from a rare moment of sobriety. Of course, if you could spare twenty bucks, I could fix that."

"Not sure I'm interested in contributing to your altered state, but I know I can get you a voucher and a place to stay for a few days. I'd even be willing to contact your family for you."

"Shit. Tell me you're not a social worker."

"Nope. Worse. A City Council member and a person who has a sister-in-law on the streets and in trouble."

"What kind of trouble?"

"The kind where people get killed."

"Is that why Shelly and Lefty took off? Shit." Tim scratched his bearded cheek. "How do I know you're really related to Shelly?"

It was a good question and one I hadn't prepared for. I displayed my driver's license to him and then used my phone to access my Facebook page. It showed that Alicia and I were married and included Alicia's full name.

That seemed to be enough for him. Tim turned and lifted several bags of clothing and other unidentifiable items from his shopping cart. He rummaged through one bag toward the bottom and brought out a book. "Shelly said family might come looking for her. She mentioned her sister's name and yours. She asked me to give you this." He hefted the book in both hands. "Got to admit it was nice having a book to read again, But I guess this belongs to you."

The book was *A Tale of Two Cities*. Damn, I thought. Alicia was right. If she was with Collins, we would have gotten the book then.

****

"I talked Tim into accepting a voucher and a ride to the hotel," I explained to Alicia as I finished up my tale of the underpass encampment. I gave her the book.

Alicia laid Michelle's book in her lap. We sat on the couch with Ginger stretched out between us. Alicia fondled Ginger's ears while I stroked her back. Ginger's purrs made it clear we were doing an acceptable job.

I added, "I didn't give him money. I think he was serious about changing his sobriety status as soon as possible."

Alicia stopped petting Ginger and turned the book over in her hands. "Michelle's favorite book. Why would she give it up? She always took it with her, no matter where she ran off to. Why would she leave this for me? So I'd know it was her?"

"Maybe. There's a letter inside. For you." I'd seen and read the note but hadn't removed it from the book.

Alicia fanned the pages of the jacketed hardback and found the single sheet of paper stuck about a third of the way through.

Dear Allie,
If you have this then that means you're still looking for

me. Lefty said you would. I was hoping you'd listen and back off. You're going to lead them to me and that means I'll be dead, too.

This is not a game. The less you know about it, the better. I don't want to endanger you or Kate or the kids. Especially not the kids.

Lefty's helping me stay safe. I'll contact you when the boogeyman is taken care of. Until then, quit looking for me.

I love you, little Sis.

Alicia stared at the short missive for much longer than it should take to read the few paragraphs.

I broke into her reverie. "What do you want to do?"

The lines around Alicia's eyes and mouth deepened. Her shoulders sagged. She looked as if the walls of our house collapsed and she was having to hold the ceiling up by herself.

The sight ripped my heart from my chest.

I wrapped my arms around her and whispered, "You're not alone in this. We're going to do this together. Like always."

Alicia took several deep breaths then eased away from me. Steel was in her eyes. "I'm going to call Keesha and have her come by. I'll show her the letter and explain why I'm taking her off the case."

Alicia didn't know it, but if she took Collins off the case, then she hit the switch on the starting gate for this old race horse. I was determined to get to the finish line before the police and before Michelle's boogeyman.

And I knew where to start.

Chapter Twenty-Three

While Alicia called Collins, I retreated to my study. I snapped up my legal pad. On it were separate pages for each of the major and minor players, along with one each for Highland Medical, Animals First, the homeless shelter, Premier Cleaning Services, and the Humane Society. I added to each list every item of new information. I leaned back and surveyed my work. Arrows and underlining took their place alongside the lists of facts and conjectures.

I then opened my email, hoping for more ammunition to add to the pages from my former paralegal. Lily was her usual efficient self. A preliminary report waited in my inbox.

Highland Medical showed no marks against it in terms of reported animal abuse or negative environmental impact findings. Since it opened less than two years ago, I thought the company hadn't been around long enough to run into any real trouble. There were citizen complaints that Lily detailed, but the Office of Laboratory Welfare (or OLAW, as Lily helpfully added) that investigated the complaints didn't cite the company. Highland's financial records were not available, but Lily noted that two new IND's were filed with the FDA in the last month. I wondered if one of those was the investigational new drug that Thompson was sure would help enrich the city's coffers.

One tidbit about the company caught my attention. Due to a spate of threatening letters received seven months ago, Highland paid for all of its senior staff to get a concealed-weapons permit from the County of Santa Barbara. The letters were turned over to the police, and the permits were granted. I thought of what Carlotti said about Dr. Sloan having an empty holster on his body. It probably held his concealed weapon. But no gun was found on the scene. According to Carlotti, at least. But that source was suspect at best.

Dr. Kyle Hench had a clean record with the police and the medical board. He was married with two children and lived in a multimillion-dollar home in the Montecito area, but that part of town was not out of line with his reported salary from the firm. He owned several investment properties, including a ranch in the Santa Barbara hills and a spread in Brazil.

Lily couldn't uncover any evidence of Dr. Ingrid Olsson moving or leaving town. She owned a house in the Mission district. That house was not on the market, and she hadn't rented or bought anything in the Palo Alto area where her supposed new job was. No airline or train tickets were issued in her name.

Sophia Carlotti turned out to have a trust fund that she seemed to be directing almost entirely to Animals First. The organization listed other donors, but Carlotti's money was the driver. She wasn't married and had no children. She attained the rank of Master Sergeant in the United States Marine Corps before her honorable discharge on a disability basis after eleven years of service. She earned not only a Purple Heart, but also a Silver Star, the third highest award for bravery that can be presented to a soldier. Interestingly to me, her service record included sniper training.

Mayor Thompson's public disclosure documents showed Highland Medical to be a significant donor in the last election along with three developers, two of whom I knew possessed projects before the planning board. I wondered if she would recuse herself when those came to the council for a vote. She owned a house in Porter Ranch, a rather ritzy area of Santa Barbara. She also owned a sailboat and a rental cabin near Lake Cachuma. She was a partner in a horse ranch that trained thoroughbreds. I wondered how lucrative her art career was, because she sure couldn't afford all that on a mayor's salary. Then I saw Lily's final note regarding the mayor. Thompson's ex-husband was a surgeon. He paid her spousal support as well as child support. The monthly payment total was beyond impressive.

In terms of the Moving Forward PAC, Lily found that the committee members consisted of a group of real estate developers and investors. The official papers of the PAC didn't disclose its donors, but they showed its official direct campaign donations to be at the legal limit. The mayor and two of our council members received funds from the PAC. Moving Forward also reported spending undisclosed funds for mailings and television and radio ads in support of various campaigns and issues. None of these expenditures were supposed to be coordinated with any candidate's campaign, but it's an open secret that communication between a PAC and a campaign occurs, albeit with plausible deniability built in.

I thought back to when I ran for the council seat. I remember hearing radio ads in support of Thompson and seeing at least one television commercial for her on our local news. I couldn't recall if those incorporated tag lines saying they were approved by her or not.

Lily included an update on Dr. Nathan Sloan. She discovered that his and his wife's first child died of lymphoma when she was only seven years old. I remembered Olsson's comments about Sloan's passion for finding a cure for childhood lymphoma. It suddenly made more sense.

The ring of the house phone broke my attention. I answered it and Sean Gregory from the Humane Society greeted me.

"I wanted you to know that everything's been settled with the Highland Medical animals, so your political muscle won't be needed."

"Glad to hear it. What happened?"

"They're being returned to Highland."

"What? Why? You sounded like you'd throw yourself under a bus before giving them back sick animals."

"That's just it. They're not sick. They're better. All of them. We gave them food, water, some antibiotics. Nothing unusual. The researchers from Highland were as amazed as we were."

"I thought they'd all been infected with dread diseases."

"So did I. I'm told they were at the end of a drug trial and maybe everything kicked in for them. But the Highland people were happy, and I'm working with some of them to arrange for these poor animals to be retired from testing. Seems like suffering through one disease and being cured should be more than enough for anyone. They shouldn't be infected with anything else. I think we may have some people at Highland who might listen to reason. And this couldn't have come at a better time. The Feds made a bust of an illegal animal farm in our ranch area today. You should hear about it on the news. We need the room at the shelter to house some of the smaller animals. We're working with wildlife refuge sanctuaries in the area to take the rest until the Feds figure out how to return them to the wild. If that's even possible."

"Illegal animals? Did they sneak across the border or something?"

Sean snorted. "Kate, trade in rare and endangered animals is the fifth largest criminal enterprise in the world. The Feds think it brings in over ten billion dollars a year. That lands it just behind drug trafficking and arms dealing in profitability. These animals came from South America, but they can come from all over, including Africa and Australia. Unfortunately, greed seems to be universal."

I hung up and added this twist to my list.

Alicia poked her head into my office. "Keesha's coming by in about an hour. I didn't tell her about the letter yet." Her worried frown told me that despite her concern about unintentionally bringing harm to her sister, she wasn't yet ready to release her active search for her.

I closed my legal pad and rose to give her a kiss on the forehead. "I'm heading out, but I'll be back before the hour's up. I promise."

"Where now?"

"Research," I said, airily. I needed to check in on one of my key assets. Our son.

****

"I told you about Caleb before. He's Dr. Sloan's assistant." Ben shrugged. "At least, he used to be. Anyway. Now he's in charge of overseeing the testing until they hire a new researcher."

I'd called Ben and found him at Highland Medical. Although working an extra shift, he agreed to take a break and meet me at the side of the building in a grassy area where the workers could go for fresh air and sunshine. Iron benches with wooden slats for the seat and back sat under young trees. Ben and I shared a place in the shade.

"They should hire Caleb for the job," Ben said. "He's amazing. He's got a great sense of humor. He's calm and smart and organized, and he's good at communicating. He's really clear about letting us know what needs to be done without being pushy or anything. And he really understands all parts of the testing process."

I considered this gushing praise of Caleb. "Should I ask what Caleb looks like?"

Ben reddened. "Anyway, I asked him, in a roundabout way, what he thought the chemical compounds were. He basically said that each was in one of three groups: weak versions of chemo drugs, counteragents for those drugs, and animal sedatives."

"Did he wonder why you were asking?"

"I told him I found some notes on a desk and wondered what they were. He was pissed that someone would leave papers like that around, but he didn't seem to be suspicious of me."

"That's important. I wouldn't want to get you in any trouble."

"No way. Besides, I can't be arrested 'cause we have a date in family court on Monday at four. I got the phone call half an hour ago."

I crushed him in a hug. "We'll have a few days to plan an appropriate celebration. Your mom will be pleased."

"I wish Aunt Michelle could be there, too."

"So do I." For so many reasons, I thought.

❋❋❋❋

I was returning to my car when it hit me. I turned and looked at the sweeping concrete-and-glass structure. From the street, I could see the front of the Highland Medical building, the visitor's parking lot, and the side of the outdoor break area. The loading docks, however, were at the back of the building. To access them, a person would have to drive into and through the employee parking area. No way Carlotti accidentally noticed the loading dock doors being open.

Irritation at Carlotti's consistent lying swept me.

I checked the time and saw I'd better hurry if I was going to make it home before Keesha Collins got there. I started to open my car door when another hand slammed it shut.

Zacharias Wise gripped my shoulder, twirled me around, and pushed me against the side of the car. "You've got to stop this."

Zach's eyes held the same intensity as they showed over twenty years ago when he'd threatened to kill me.

"Stop what, Zach?" I tried to keep my voice even. I didn't want the anger or fear I felt to leech out and escalate matters.

His index finger came within one inch of the tip of my nose. "Don't play the idiot. Ben is my son, and you can't steal him. You're going to stop this now."

"Or what, Zach? You planning on beating me up on this very public parking lot? Killing me? That sounds like a great way to win back Ben's loyalty."

Zach raised a gigantic fist.

A blur leapt from the right side of my eyes. Two men tackled Zach and pinned him to the asphalt. Ben cocked his own fist, but the other man grabbed it and shook his head. Ben relented.

All the fight left Zach's body. He stared up into Ben's face and burst into tears.

Both my saviors rose and dusted themselves off. As Zach lay sobbing on the ground, Ben introduced me to his fellow avenger. Caleb was an inch or two shorter than Ben but carried more muscle. His dark, curly hair formed a dense, neatly trimmed frame around an attractive square face. He was not the stereotypical science nerd. More like a tackle on the Los Angeles Rams.

"Nice to meet you, Kate," he said, and offered a broad hand for a firm handshake. "Sorry about the circumstances." He jerked his head toward Zach, who was beginning to get control of himself. "I can call the police if you like. But if you don't want to press charges, it might be a good idea if Ben and I take his dad somewhere where the two of them can talk."

I looked at Ben who was studying his father. "I think

that's a great idea, Caleb."

Ben and Caleb hauled Zach to his feet and led him back to the shade of the Highland Medical building side lawn. I felt like both Ben and Zach were in good hands.

****

I made it home minutes before Collins showed up. On the way, I decided I wasn't going to burden Alicia with news of Zach's attack yet. The tight timing of my arrival saved me from making small talk with Alicia and from feeling guilty about withholding the information from my wife.

Alicia shared the letter with Collins and explained why she wanted to drop the case.

Collins handed the letter back to Alicia. "I understand why Michelle's afraid. Looks like she did see something at Highland either during or after the murder. And she's spooked."

I agreed. "Especially if she got word that someone's been asking after her at the homeless encampments. She'd have no way of telling who was coming after her."

Alicia interrupted. "But we're the only people looking for her. Keesha told everyone she's searching for Michelle on our behalf."

Collins said, "That's not quite true." At Alicia's incredulous look, Collins clarified. "I mean, I'm looking for her and I do tell people that I'm working for her family. But not everyone asks why I'm looking for Michelle, and besides that, anyone could say they were working for you. Like that one guy who showed up at the abandoned factory asking about her."

"The one with the gun," I added. "I'm sure that piece of information got passed along to either Lefty or Michelle. That can't make them feel safe. Especially when another guy shows up at the underpass camp while they're there." I looked at Collins. "Or was it the same guy?"

"It's probable. Same general description, but with no distinguishing characteristics, and with somewhat unreliable witnesses, there's no way to know for sure."

Alicia rose and paced the living room before ending up in

front of the floor-to-ceiling glass window that was our view to the backyard and the ocean beyond. I didn't think she even noticed the crashing waves. "I can't risk leading a murderer to Michelle. I can't."

"Then let's take another route," I said. "Michelle won't be free to come back to us until whatever happened at Highland is cleared up. Why don't we work on that angle?"

I outlined the information I'd gathered regarding the murder of Dr. Sloan.

Collins took notes as I talked. She filled three pages of her notebook. "What's the motive? Who gains from Sloan's death?"

"His children are in his will. They're too young to be planning homicide, but the ex-wife could on their behalf. Especially if she has control of the money until they are of legal age. Animals First also gets a large bequest."

Collins objected. "But you said the organization doesn't need the money. Carlotti's trust fund keeps them going."

"Every charity always needs money. It's not a strong motive, maybe, but it's a possible motive."

Collins tapped a page in her notebook. "What about this money laundering? Maybe Sloan was skimming and the mob took him out."

"Could be." I looked over to Alicia who was still staring wordlessly at the ocean. We'd had a gruesome experience with a mob hit. A man was thrown off our backyard cliff. Not an experience we ever wanted repeated. "Or maybe he got back into hock with the loan sharks and they decided to kill him for repeated infractions." I flipped through my mental notes. I hadn't told Alicia or Collins about the list of medications or other papers I found in the Animals First office. I wasn't sure how Collins would feel about such tainted bits of evidence, but I knew Alicia would be angry I'd involved Ben in something risky by asking him about the drugs. In any case, I couldn't see how anything we learned tied into those pieces of paper.

"If it's loan sharks, murdering someone in their place of employment is a new tactic. They usually break legs in the privacy of the person's home or a back alley." Collins closed her notebook. "So, am I off the hunt for Michelle? Do you want me to check into anything else? Or should I send you a final bill?"

"No." Alicia turned from the window. "I've changed my mind. Kate's right. We've got to find Michelle. She's either seen the killer or knows something about them. And they're looking for her. So are the police. She won't be safe until she's home with us. You've got to find her. Now."

Collins's phone beeped. She poked at it, and her eyes scanned the screen. "Looks like we might have company looking for her. Your sister has been officially declared a person of interest in the murder of Nathan Sloan."

Chapter Twenty-Four

We opened the online link for the local news. An unflattering, old DMV photo of Michelle topped the story. In it, she was described as being mentally ill, armed, and possibly dangerous. For now, her relation to Alicia was not part of the news story.

"Shit." Alicia collapsed into a chair. "Trigger-happy nut cases will be after her now."

"I'm heading out," Collins said. "And I'll be doubly careful no one follows me. I'll keep an eye out for anyone else asking questions around the camps." She gathered her notebook and laptop.

I accompanied her to the door. She turned to me before leaving. "Text me if anything comes up. Anything."

Alicia was on the phone as I entered the living room. She mouthed Sarah's name at me.

"Yes, we saw the news. The police are wrong. Your aunt is not involved." Alicia listened silently for a minute before rolling her eyes and punching the Speaker button.

Sarah's voice filled the room. "...can't believe you're so calm about this. Don't you care?"

I broke in. "Hey. You have no idea what your mother's been going through. I told you we've been looking for Michelle, and we'll continue to do that. So, knock it off."

Sarah was silent. Admittedly, it was out of character for me to snap at her, but I was also out of patience.

"By the way," I added. "Did you tell Zach where Ben worked?"

"Why?"

"Because he showed up at Highland Medical this afternoon while I was there and threatened to beat me to a pulp. He couldn't have known Ben worked at Highland unless you told him."

Sarah's voice was small. "He wouldn't have hurt you."

"Oh, yes he would. He was about to belt me when Ben and a friend of his knocked him down and sat on him." I heard Alicia gasp, but I didn't stop. "Why did you tell Zach about Ben's work?"

"I...I thought it might help him. To talk to Ben directly without you or Mom around to, like, influence him."

Alicia burst out. "You idiot. Influence Ben? You think this adoption was our idea? Ben came to us and asked, not the other way around. I know you're not a fan of this, but it has nothing to do with you, so suck it up. And as for your father, I have never, in all the time you were growing up, said one bad thing about him. Not when he missed your birthdays or holidays. Not when he stopped visiting you. Not when he didn't write or call or even pay child support. Never. And there were a lot of things I might have said. You have no idea what I put up with. More than I ever should have. It was only when you kids were in danger that I left him. You don't know all that went on. You probably shouldn't." Alicia took a breath. "If you choose to have a relationship with that man, that's on your head. But don't you ever, ever again drag any of us, including your brother, into your dealings with him. Do you understand? Do you?"

Sarah's voice grew tight. "I'm sorry, Mom. I was only trying to help. Zach's wife called me. She's worried about him. He lost his job last month. He took it hard, and he's been acting all weird. She wanted him to go to counseling, but he refused. She said this whole issue with Ben and the adoption seemed to put him over the edge. It's gotten so bad, she took the kids and left. I thought if he could talk to Ben, maybe..."

Alicia rubbed her face with her hands. Her mouth opened and closed twice before she shook her head and turned away.

I took a calming breath. "Did it occur to you that telling an unbalanced man the whereabouts of the source of his anger might have bad consequences?"

Quiet sobbing came over the line. "I screwed up. I'm so sorry. Is Ben all right? Are you all right?"

"Yes, we're both fine. But you need to get it through your head that Zach can be dangerous. He needs help, but not the kind you can give him." I hung up.

Alicia wrapped her arms around me from behind. "I

swear, I don't know what to do with that child."

I turned in her arms and hugged her in return. We stood together, a safe cocoon in the midst of a whirling tornado of chaos.

****

Sometimes, before the trial of a major case, I would lean back in my chair and let the whole court case play out in my head. Arguments, counter arguments, and possible questions all rolled through my thoughts in technicolor.

I tried that with the murder of Dr. Sloan, from the moment of Michelle's cleaning crew entering the building through her leaving Highland, gun drawn. I added various scenarios of Carlotti's actions in the immediate aftermath of the murder, then wound the film back and tried to imagine what might have led up to the murder itself. A picture of the animals that were stolen then ultimately returned to Highland Medical kept inserting itself in the scenarios.

I considered what Hench told me about the murder taking place in his lab. Why was Nathan Sloan in Kyle Hench's lab? Was Sloan the intended victim or a bystander? Was Hench the one in danger now?

A hand on my shoulder broke my reverie.

"A counter-offer came in on that place near the college. Can you do without me for a couple of hours?" Alicia sounded exhausted and her eyes were red.

"Are you feeling up to that?"

"No, but the alternative is to sit around worrying or run off and do something stupid like smack Zach or chase down the people who are making Michelle's life even more miserable than it already is."

When Alicia left, I checked my email and found one from Johnson. He wrote that he suspected a possible conspiracy involving officials in the city government. He didn't want to get into details in writing, but could I meet him later to discuss the issue?

Unlike the phone message, I didn't delete it, but I didn't answer it either. I wanted to find out more about John Johnson before engaging with him again. In the meantime, there were more important things I needed to do.

****

I dropped off letters addressed to Alexander Garland at the shelter where Michelle stayed and at the underpass encampment. My last stop was the abandoned warehouse where I first met Alexander, alias Lefty. I came bearing sandwiches and chips, which generated a positive welcome from the people settled in the shade of the building.

As I handed out the refreshments, I asked if anyone else was inquiring after Lefty.

"Not Lefty," one man with a buzz cut said. He displayed tattoos of parrots down one arm and skulls down the other. The tats were memorable. I'd seen this same man the first time I visited the encampment. He seemed to recognize me as well. "His girlfriend sure is popular, though."

"You mean, Shelly? How so?"

"Tall, Black woman came asking after her a couple of times, and a swanky guy came by once. Police stopped by, too. This chick, Shelly, has got some serious people after her mighty fine tail."

I figured the police would check out all the known homeless hangouts. And Collins was earning her fee. But who was the other guy? "You said a swanky guy came by?"

"Yeah. Swanky. I mean, he wore a baseball cap and polo shirt and all, but his shoes were all leather and shiny. That guy was no jock."

"Did you tell him anything?"

"Who, me? Uh-uh. No way. I ain't about to get my ass kicked by Lefty. Let me tell you, that man is a good friend, but a very nasty enemy."

I held out my letter with a twenty-dollar bill on top. "If you see Lefty or Shelly again, would you please give them this? There's fifty dollars more for you if Lefty tells me you were the first one to reach him with this note."

Both items disappeared into his back pocket. "I'll be sure to give it to Lefty if I see him again. But you know that man's a wanderer. Might have left the state by now. By the way, next time you bring sandwiches, make sure they add extra mayo. They're a little dry."

As I started to leave, tattoo man shouted, "Hey, Swanky Guy was driving a silver Lexus. Personalized plates."

****

I texted Collins about the other man on Michelle's trail even though I knew the car description could cover a quarter of the people living in Santa Barbara. I'd already let her know I was handing out letters to Lefty asking him to bring Michelle to either our house or to contact Collins for a safe location where we could guard them both. I had no way of knowing if any of the letters would reach Lefty or if he would comply, but I felt obligated to try.

Ready for part two of my plan, I headed for the downtown criminal courts building and my friend, Quentin Jefferson. When I called, Quentin was about to close up his office for the day, but he agreed to stay late to see me.

On my drive over, Collins called in response to my text.

"I know the man you're calling Swanky Guy," she said. "He's a P.I. by the name of Peter Nevin."

I thought for a moment about who else besides us would hire a private investigator. The list was short and chilling. "Do you think Sloan's murderer saw Michelle and is tracking her down?"

"Maybe. Nevin is known for his high fees and his willingness to bend rules whatever way his clients want."

"Bend, but not break?"

"There are rumors. He almost lost his license once. But he got off. His clients for that particular case provided a lawyer who had a very convincing way with the judge."

I thought of Quentin Jefferson and wondered if he knew about this. "Bribes?"

"That's one way the mob works."

Chapter Twenty-Five

The county courthouse was an impressive Spanish Colonial Revival-style building with a clock tower and the ubiquitous Santa Barbara red tile roof. Even though it was completed in 1929, its façade looked as white and fresh as the year it was built, thanks to a major project that restored the four-building complex to its original grandeur. I experienced no trouble finding a spot for my car since the parking lot was nearly empty. Most of the court reporters, clerks, and bailiffs had already departed for the day.

My years as a trial attorney made court buildings seem like second homes, but it felt strange to stride along the tiled courthouse hallway and have my steps echo in empty corridors.

Quentin Jefferson's wood-paneled office was spacious, as befitted a Superior Court judge. Despite the apparent emptiness of the building, I made sure to close his office door after I entered. He raised an eyebrow but didn't comment. Instead, he greeted me with a hearty handshake and a half hug. We both sat in armchairs on the visitors' side of his desk. "You were mysterious on the phone. What's up that I needed to postpone my journey home?"

I filled him in on Michelle's new status as suspect number one as far as the police were concerned. He didn't seem surprised at this, which gave me hope he knew something he would share. I also told him of Collins's identification of Peter Nevin and his involvement in the search for Michelle.

Quentin crossed his legs and leaned back. "I've heard the rumors about Nevin, but nothing's ever been proven."

"Any hints that he or his lawyer bribed a judge?"

"Yes, and it makes me sick because I'm sure it's true. I'm sorry to say that bad apple is still sitting on the bench. Several of us pushed for an ethics investigation when the rumors started, but someone was very slick. No evidence was ever uncovered." Quentin cocked his head. "But you could have asked me that over the phone."

"That was a side bit that dropped in my lap on my way over. What I really want to know is if you've heard any rumors as to who told the police that Michelle carried a gun with her when she was at Highland Medical that night."

Quentin rubbed his jaw. I waited.

He cleared his throat. "You know I can't comment on an ongoing investigation, especially to a relative of a suspect. It's one thing to chat with you when you weren't involved. Another thing entirely now."

"I know. That's why I wanted to do this in person."

Quentin rubbed his jaw harder. "Sometimes I do hear things. But they're not official. And even if I heard a name from an unofficial source, I couldn't disclose that to you. But I can't see the legal jeopardy in telling you I heard there might have been an anonymous tip phoned in."

"The police issued *a person of interest* announcement based on an anonymous tip? I find that hard to believe."

"Agreed. They would need corroborating evidence. Say, something like security footage that might be too blurry to make an identification but clear enough to possibly match someone's description once they got a name. In theory, that is."

****

My long and adventurous day made me want to sit out by the ocean and let my overworked brain have a chance to cool off. It was not to be. Ben's car was in the driveway, and Alicia's car was in the garage. Forced to park on the street, I steeled myself for more human interaction.

To my surprise, Caleb was with Ben and Alicia in the living room.

Ben said, "We were filling Mom in on Zach. We haven't gotten very far, so you didn't miss much." Ben described his conversation with Zach after I left and how Caleb played mediator between the two men. "If Caleb hadn't been there, I swear I would have slugged Zach several times in the whole argument."

Caleb disagreed. "Actually, it wasn't much of an argument. Zach was pretty beaten down emotionally by the time we talked. He looked like he could barely form sentences let alone argue with anyone."

"Zach told us he lost his job," Ben said, "and that his wife left him. He said my adoption was a big 'screw you' to him when he was down, only he didn't use those exact words."

"Anyway, Ben convinced Zach to come with us to Cottage Hospital," Caleb said.

Ben nudged him. "It was more like Caleb talked him into it."

"Whatever." Caleb elbowed Ben back. "The important thing is, Zach agreed to a voluntary hospitalization. They took him in on an emergency basis for a pysch eval, and we're hoping the program will accept him for treatment."

Ben added, "They treat vets, and they even have an in-patient psychiatric unit if they decide he needs that."

"Yep. Hopefully, this will get him the help he needs," Caleb said. He fist-bumped Ben. "We make a good team."

As the two boys beamed at each other, Alicia and I shared a knowing look.

"Oh, one other thing," Caleb said. "Ben kind of filled me in on what's been going on. He asked me about Dr. Sloan's research and if there were any problems or anything. I got to thinking. A couple of days before the doc was killed, I went in to say congrats on the newest treatment getting promoted to clinical trials so quickly. I mean, we treated those animals for over five months and were all really jazzed that this combination of drugs... Well, the details aren't important. But when I went into his office, he'd just hung up the phone. He looked worried. I asked him what was wrong. He put his head in his hands and muttered something about not knowing what to do. He mentioned the FDA, but I didn't know if they were the ones on the phone or what."

"The Federal Drug Administration?" I puzzled over that before asking, "Did he ever clarify what was going on?"

"No, but I also remember him mentioning a name. I didn't know the person, so it didn't register with me at that point. But when Ben told me about this and all the people involved, I recalled Sloan saying that name. He said, 'Damn Carlotti.'"

Chapter Twenty-Six

Another almost sleepless night led to a groggy morning for me. I dragged myself out of bed and headed for the shower. I hoped the hot water would stimulate the few brain cells I had left into some form of activity. After only a moment under a blissful heated waterfall, my meditation was interrupted by a tapping on the shower enclosure. I cracked the door open, and Alicia informed me that our P.I. was on the phone wanting to talk with both of us.

"I've got possible leads on Lefty," Collins informed us. She outlined her search through Marine Corps records for people who served with Sergeant Alexander "Lefty" Garland. She'd called all of those who lived in the Santa Barbara area to see if they'd heard from him. "None of the ones I talked to admitted to having contact with Lefty in years. Only two didn't answer their phones yesterday. They didn't return my call either. I'll drive by their homes. Check for any activity. If I have to, I'll surveil the houses and wait for them to get home from work."

"Since there are two houses to check out, do you want me to sit on one while you watch the other?" Alicia asked. "Lord knows I've spent a lot of time looking at houses."

"That's probably not a good idea," Collins said. "Once Kate tipped me off that Nevin was looking for Michelle, too, I asked two of my associates to keep an eye on both of you. Alicia, you're clear, but someone's tailing Kate."

Collins signed off and Alicia slammed her coffee cup on the kitchen table. "That's it," she said. "You're staying home. No massages. No council business. And definitely no looking for Michelle."

"If I'm being followed, it means I'm close to finding out what's going on."

"No, it doesn't. It means you're close to getting yourself or Michelle killed." Alicia gave me the ancient death stare.

It's the one teachers perfect in order to control their unruly students. "I'm going to the police department and tell Detective Levine everything that's been going on, including Peter Nevin's involvement and the fact that you're being followed. You, on the other hand, are going to stay here and not move."

I re-tied the belt of my robe and adjusted the towel on my wet hair as I considered Alicia's plans and demands. "I hear you're concerned—"

"Concerned? I'm not concerned. I'm terrified. Michelle is missing and being chased by who knows what kind of monsters. Zach is off his head and attacking you and Ben. And now you're being targeted by people who are involved in very illegal activities, including, it seems, death and dismemberment." Tears sprouted from her eyes. "I can't control whether or not you have a heart attack, but I should have some say over whether you stupidly throw your body in front of a speeding train."

I reached for her hand, but she pulled it away.

"I'm getting dressed, and then I'm going to the police station." She marched out of the room.

Fifteen minutes later, Alicia slammed out of the house without saying goodbye. She was back within minutes. "My damn car has a dead battery. I'm taking yours."

It took a moment for that to sink in, and I yelled, "Wait," at the recently slammed door. Despite my less-than-dressed condition, I sprinted out the door and down the driveway. I saw my car roaring away halfway down the block. I scanned the area, but no other cars appeared to follow her.

I pulled my robe more tightly around me as I walked back to the house. As relieved as I was to know no one seemed to be interested in tailing Alicia even though she was in my car, I wasn't about to sit at home for safety's sake. I considered my options. Alicia knew I didn't respond well to edicts. On the other hand, I felt no desire to add more stress to her already overburdened life. I chewed on my cheek considering if Alicia's words left any wiggle room.

I dried my hair, got dressed, and flipped open my computer. In deference to Alicia, I contacted the chairs of two subcommittees and informed them I wouldn't be at the sessions today. I also called my fellow council member

Reynaldo Sanchez and asked him to fill in for me at a meet-and-greet business luncheon. I checked and cleared all my constituent emails as well.

After I'd done my duty to my community and my wife, I opened an email from my former paralegal.

Lily did some follow-up investigations on Premier Cleaning Services. The company was cited for not providing workers with personal protective gear when cleaning hazardous areas and for a lack of thorough vetting of its employees. The last one explained to me how Michelle was hired so quickly. A complete background check would have turned up her police record in Nevada that included vagrancy and minor drug possession, surely a block to employment that required a security clearance.

Nothing further turned up on Ingrid Olsson per se. But police in Morro Bay found a car registered to her. It was stripped and abandoned. Morro Bay was on the coastal route to the San Francisco area, which meant that Olsson could have driven it up there on her way to her supposed new job at Exeter. But if she did, why didn't she file a stolen car report? The suspicions I'd been forming regarding Olsson intensified exponentially.

The intrepid reporter, John Johnson, Jr., was born and raised in Laguna Beach and attended Cal State Long Beach where he earned a bachelor's in communication. He worked in several local political campaigns as a speechwriter before taking a job with the *Laguna Beach Independent* and then the *Orange County Register*. He moved to Santa Barbara and joined the local paper five months ago. Lily noted that he'd lived with his parents after college while he was involved in politics. He only moved out when he got the job with the *Register*. His father died of cancer nine months ago, but his mother still lived in the family home in Laguna Beach. Four parking violations, two speeding tickets, and a youthful brush with marijuana were the sum total of Johnson's police record.

Lily uncovered an IRS investigation into an old political action committee fined for illegal campaign contributions. The item of note was that the parent companies for Highland Medical were two of the corporations behind that political action committee. In fact, many of the same players in that closed PAC were the ones who formed Moving Forward, the organization that pooled campaign contributions in support of our dear mayor, Julia Thompson.

Lily added a note at the bottom of her report. John Johnson, Sr., took part in a trial for an investigational new drug to treat his lung cancer. The new drug was developed at Highland Medical.

I mulled this over as I microwaved some leftovers for lunch. If Johnson suspected his father's death was caused by the treatment rather than the cancer, it would give him an excellent reason to bear a grudge against Highland. I flipped on the TV while I ate. The local noon news came on with reports on the continued protests over the ground squirrel issue in Shoreline Park along with some of the recommended measures the council was now studying. I didn't see my granddaughter, in costume or otherwise, taking part in the latest demonstration, which made me hope that Sarah was mollified by the proposal I developed.

As Sean Gregory from the Humane Society predicted, the story of a raid on an animal farm in the mountains made the news. Overcrowded cages with baby ocelots, chimpanzees, pythons, and scarlet macaws filled the screen. The reporter described the number of animals as one of the largest hauls of illegally imported exotic and endangered animals in the history of the U.S. Fish and Wildlife Service. The operation had, reportedly, been sending out over one hundred animals each week to various distribution centers around Southern California where they were purchased by private collectors.

"The government warns that not only are all of these animals endangered by removing them from the wild and keeping them in homes, but they are also a danger to humans. Wild animals can attack their owners. They also carry diseases that can be fatal to us." The wide-eyed reporter continued, reading from a list, "These include rabies, distemper, herpes, salmonella, polio, tuberculosis, Rocky Mountain spotted fever, and the bubonic plague. Wild animals have parasites as well, such as intestinal worms and protozoa, that can spread to humans."

The report triggered a memory. I shut off the television and headed to my wall safe. I pulled out the papers I'd copied from the ones in Sophia Carlotti's office and found the page detailing the purchases from an animal breeding service. I ran my finger down the list of delivery dates for the animals. A shipment was scheduled for the night Dr. Nathan Sloan was murdered. The next delivery date was set for this evening.

I called the trucking company listed on my purloined invoice. I pretended to be from Highland Medical and inquired about the delivery time for the order. Having the purchase order number must have helped since the receptionist didn't question my request.

The helpful woman checked her computer and said, "A Dr. Hench called and asked that the delivery time be moved up to six o'clock this evening. Is that still the case? If not, I need to know so that I can contact the driver."

I assured her that the new time would be fine.

"And is there still a pick-up with that?"

I agreed to that, too, and hung up.

Would the police check out the delivery on my say-so? Doubtful. I had less than six hours to figure out a compelling reason for them to take a look.

While I was contemplating how to circumvent Alicia's orders and arrange to be present when that delivery was made to Highland Medical, I got a text from Alicia. My guilty conscience leapt to the conclusion that she could read my thoughts from afar and was intervening before I could ignore her instructions. As it was, she tersely informed me that she was having lunch with a friend and then heading to her office. She'd be home very late.

I took that to mean she was still scared and angry and trying to allow herself time to calm down. Given all that happened, I was surprised she thought that merely a day away might settle things down for her.

I wandered into our driveway and looked up and down Shoreline Drive. Cars lined the side of the road, and a few looked to be occupied. I calculated the odds. I was pretty sure if Collins and company were right about the tail, then that person was more interested in knowing where I was going than in stopping me, permanently. After all, in the past day or so, anyone following me had ample opportunity to corner me or otherwise do me harm. Of course, there's a huge gap between "pretty sure" and certain. And Alicia would be quite annoyed if I ended up in the hospital because of that gap. I wouldn't be too pleased, myself.

I texted Collins and asked if her operative was still watching over me. She sent back an affirmative, so I decided to take a stroll up and down a few blocks to see if anything happened. Collins wasn't happy but promised to let her colleague know my plan.

Half a block from my house, I spotted a shiny silver Lexus with a man in the driver's seat. My eyes met his dark ones in the sideview mirror of the car before he shifted his gaze to something in the seat beside him.

I strolled past the car and then pulled my phone out of my pocket. As I talked to the nonexistent caller, I turned and glanced at the driver through the front windshield. He wore sunglasses, a baseball cap, and polo shirt. I couldn't see if he was wearing spiffy shoes or not, but he otherwise fit the description of the swanky Peter Nevin.

As I'd hoped, he didn't leap out of his car and attack me. In fact, he turned his face away as I paced back and forth. I figured it would be good for me to be able to spot his car if he did follow me, so I noted his license plate. It was a vanity plate. I repeated it to myself as I faux-chatted on the phone and hurried back home.

Before I reached home, my phone rang for real. Although Ben's number was on the screen, Caleb's voice sounded in my ear.

"Hi, Kate. Ben loaned me his phone to call you. I heard something strange, and we thought you might want to know."

I tucked the phone between my ear and my shoulder and unlocked the front door as I listened.

Caleb said, "One of Dr. Hench's research assistants is a buddy of mine. We were talking, and he told me he thought some of the animals we got back from the Humane Society weren't the same ones we treated in the lab."

I seized a pen and paper and scribbled down Nevin's license plate number before I could forget. Then I turned my brain to what Caleb was trying to tell me. "You mean the Humane Society gave you the wrong animals? Like cats instead of dogs?"

"No. Some of the mice and two of the rabbits were not the ones my friend worked with. You get to know the animals pretty well. Even the mice can have different characteristics that make them recognizable."

"Maybe a mix-up happened, and they gave you the wrong mice."

"I suggested that, but the guy said he went back to the shelter and asked. There were no other mice at the shelter. No rabbits either. The week before our animals arrived, the shelter held a big adoption fair, so their place was somewhat empty. No possibility that they mixed up the ones in our cages with any of their own."

"Did he tell Hench?"

"He did. Hench told him he was being ridiculous. In fact, the doc got a little nasty with my buddy. Said he'd certainly know his own animals especially since he personally worked with all those animals in the last week. He reamed my friend a new one for even suggesting that the ones we got back weren't the ones that belonged to the lab."

"Sounds like Hench is a man who doesn't like to be wrong about anything." A new thought struck me. "What did you mean when you said Hench was working with the animals personally in the last week. Didn't he usually work in his lab?"

"Dr. Hench sets up the experiments, but his research assistants and lab techs carry them out. It's only toward the end of the trials that he takes over. He does everything himself at that point. No one's even allowed into the lab. He says he needs to be the point person so he can accurately write up the results. Guess he's a little anal."

"That does sound a bit obsessive. But he's the one who writes up the applications to the FDA for human trials. Maybe he needs to be extra careful at that point." I thought about why the looks of the animals might change. "The Humane Society gave the animals fluids and antibiotics. And they got better. Maybe the tech didn't recognize them when they were healthy."

"Maybe." Caleb didn't sound convinced, and neither was I.

As I clicked to end the call, Sophia Carlotti came to

mind. She removed the animals from the lab. Would she have a reason to keep some and substitute others?

I tried calling her, but, as usual, she didn't answer. I left a message asking her to call me, but I held little hope that would happen.

Ginger came into the kitchen, crying for attention. Or food. With her it was hard to tell. I picked her up and cuddled her while I theorized aloud about Highland Medical and Michelle. I presented opening arguments to my jury of one kitty regarding the murder of Nathan Sloan and the involvement of Michelle Mazer. I took her purrs to mean she agreed with me. I sat at the table and placed the contented cat on my lap.

The newspaper lay on the table where Alicia placed it early this morning before Collins's call. I unfolded it and saw a follow-up article on Nathan Sloan's death. The autopsy report showed the cause of death to be a nine-millimeter bullet. According to the newspaper, Sloan was licensed to own a Smith & Wesson M&P Shield 9mm for concealed-carry purposes. According to police, no gun was found in the lab. The article didn't mention anything about the holster that Carlotti said she'd seen on his body.

Michelle was named as a person of interest in the ongoing investigation. The article described her as having a history of homelessness and mental illness that dated back to her early adulthood, which made me wonder where they got that piece of information. As far as I knew, only Collins and the police knew about that. Were the police deliberately leaking bits of information such as Michelle's medical history and her possession of a gun?

The article also covered the history of Highland Medical in Santa Barbara. Kyle Hench was quoted as extolling the incredible progress the research center made in the year and a half they'd been operating. He noted the two previous investigational new drugs the company had gotten approved and credited Nathan Sloan by name as one of the key contributors to a new drug protocol to treat B-Cell lymphoma that would soon be submitted to the Federal Drug Administration for human testing approval.

Mention was made of the ongoing controversy of using

animals in testing and the threats made against the staff of Highland by "animal rights extremists."

A red flag waved vigorously in my mind. I placed the sleeping kitty on Alicia's chair and went to get my notes in my office. I skimmed over what Hench told me the first time we met regarding the development of new drugs.

I called Ben. When I asked, he put me on hold until he could locate Caleb, who was in another lab.

"Hi, Kate," Caleb said. "Ben tells me you have a question."

"Yes. When you told me Dr. Sloan took a phone call that he was upset about, you mentioned something about congratulating him on a quick approval for a drug he developed."

"Yeah. A derivative of methotrexate that lessened side effects and improved survival rates for B-cell lymphoma. It was a pet project of his."

"How much time did it take to develop and test that drug?"

"That's hard to say. A research company owns the rights to any research a doctor does while in their employ. Dr. Sloan joined Highland right when it opened, like I did. I was assigned to him from the beginning. It seemed like he'd been thinking about this twist on methotrexate for a while, but I don't know if he'd done any experiments on it at his old work. I mean, he shouldn't have built on work he did for another company, but I can't say for sure that he didn't. Anyway, we started work on it from day one. There are a lot of steps before the fine tuning of the drug, but from the time we began and the time we handed it over for final tests with Dr. Hench, it was probably fifteen months, which is pretty fast. Hench was able to replicate our results and verify the protocols in under three months." Caleb paused. "Come to think of it, that's kind of odd."

"What is?"

"I'd have to check my lab records to be sure, but I think our final test subjects required almost five months of infusions for the lymphoma to become dormant. Dr. Hench must have made some adjustments to get the same outcomes in only three months. I wonder what they were?"

I had an inkling and it wasn't pretty.

Chapter Twenty-Seven

I spent the next few hours delving into medical research practices and procedures. I was still in the midst when Carlotti actually returned my telephone call.

Knowing Carlotti's limited patience for small talk, I jumped straight to my concern. "Did you keep any of the animals you took out of the lab?"

"Why would I keep them?"

"Because they were proof of animal abuse."

Carlotti scoffed. "That'd be a good idea if I weren't concerned about being hauled up on charges of breaking and entering and grand theft."

"You could hide the theft by substituting other animals for the ones you took."

A moment of silence ensued on Carlotti's end of the call. "Damn. I wish I'd thought of that. Maybe next time."

I couldn't tell if she was being sincere or ironic. I switched topics. "The day before he was killed, Nathan Sloan was chatting on the phone, possibly with the FDA, and your name was mentioned."

Carlotti sounded suspicious. "My name? Why?"

"I was hoping you could help me with that. What was he doing that the FDA might be interested in?"

"As far as I know, Sloan wasn't doing anything the FDA would be involved in. At least, Jeff didn't tell me he suspected anything like that. Rat-faced Sloan was only weaseling out of our agreement with him to phase out animal testing. Jeff found out that spineless creep kept ordering more and more animals when he swore he was going to cut back to half of what they usually bought. That's what I went there to talk to him about that night."

"Did you call the meeting or did he?"

"I told the jackass that I needed to see him. He set up the time and place. Said he was glad I called and that he wanted to show me something. I figured he'd want to try to gloss over what he was doing, show me smoke and mirrors about how it was all really wonderful, and I wasn't understanding the big picture. But I wasn't going to let that back-stabbing animal killer pull any crap."

"I'm guessing that means you brought a gun with you."

"Of course, I brought my gun. Any sane person who deals with these slime bags takes precautions."

I skipped the next logical question and pivoted instead. "I have a list of delivery orders for test animals. You said Sloan was increasing the amounts. Do you know how frequently Highland was receiving animals?"

"Usually, it was once every two or three months. But Jeff found proof they were coming more frequently. What's your list say?"

"About every two weeks. In fact, one's due tonight." I thought of a question Alicia had asked a week ago. "When you got to Highland, were there any other cars in the parking lot?"

"Only one. A dark sedan that belonged to Sloan. I'd seen it before."

"Did you see anyone or any other vehicle leaving before you drove up to the loading dock?"

"Only the big rig in the driveway."

"Was the truck empty or full?"

"How the hell am I supposed to know? I didn't do a stop and search on it."

I tried to hide my exasperation. "Did the truck seem to ride heavy or light?"

Carlotti paused for a moment, as if in thought. "I did see it go over one of those traffic bumps in the street. It didn't jitterbug all over the place, so my guess would be it carried a load."

"Jitterbug?"

"Yeah. You know, hop and jiggle all over the place like an empty rig does when it hits a pothole. It was one of the things we looked for when a truck was coming our way in the Mideast."

"What about the speed of the truck?"

"It was in a hurry. It pulled out of the driveway quickly

and took the right onto the street a little too fast. It leaned quite a bit on that curve."

So far, all of her tale verified my theories. I pushed for one last piece. "Did Jeffrey ever say Sloan mentioned a concern over the types of animals being ordered for the lab? Something that wasn't the usual test subject?"

An ominous silence grew on Carlotti's side of the phone. When she finally spoke, anger exploded through her words. "So, that's why they increased deliveries. That whole Highland Medical torture chamber is a bigger pile of shit than Jeff or I suspected. Not only did Sloan turn out to be a traitor, but now you're telling me that Highland is importing endangered animals?"

I heard what sounded like the slide of a gun chambering rounds.

"The wrong guy died. I'm going to kill that bastard, Hench."

"Sophia! Hang on!" But I was yelling into dead air.

Chapter Twenty-Eight

I snatched up my keys and barreled out to the garage before I remembered that Alicia was using my car, and a warped private investigator was waiting to follow me. I cursed and then called Ben. "I need a ride to Highland. Quickly."

"Sure. Caleb is with me. We'll be right over."

"No. Don't come here. I'll meet you at the parking lot for Shoreline Park in fifteen minutes."

I flew down the treacherous Thousand Steps, then sprinted as quickly as I could over the compacted wet sand and along the base of the tall cliffs until I reached the staircase for the park. I was breathing heavily by the time I mounted the staircase and entered the parking lot.

Ben and Caleb were waiting for me. I huffed a greeting to the two men and hopped into the back. As we drove, I outlined the situation, although I left out the part about hearing the sound of a gun slide from Carlotti's side of the conversation. I didn't want to panic them, or me.

"I tried to reach Hench, but he isn't answering his phone. I need to make sure Sophia doesn't do anything more stupid than she's already done. If I can stop her, maybe we don't have to involve the police."

Caleb turned to stare at me from the front seat. He regarded me with a calm, but serious, expression. "And if you can't stop her?"

"Then it's your job to call in the cavalry."

Carlotti's van was not in the front of Highland, so I directed Ben around back. The parking lot was nearly empty. We spotted Carlotti's van pulled up to the loading dock behind Hench's lab. A red Model S Tesla was parked beside it. The door to the loading dock was slid open about two feet.

Caleb pointed at the door. "That's supposed to be closed and locked."

I shared my guesses with him. "Hench is expecting a delivery. I bet he unlocks it in advance. And if Carlotti couldn't get in the front door after hours, I'm sure she would have checked out the back way in."

I directed them to stay in the car and crept up the outside stairs to the loading platform. I snuck a peek though the opening. Kyle Hench and Sophia Carlotti were yelling at each other from across the lab. I looked back to the car and made a hand motion telling Ben and Caleb to call the police. I prayed they understood. I slipped inside.

Hench whirled to face me. "What the hell are you doing here?"

I pointed to Carlotti. "Ms. Carlotti has made some very troubling accusations against you and Highland."

"This bitch is a troublemaker and a nut case," Hench said.

"Possibly. I know she lied about what happened the night Nathan Sloan was killed."

Carlotti swung her head in my direction. "What are you talking about?"

I bent my head toward the cargo doors. "There's no way the story you told me can be true. You said you were driving by Highland and saw the loading dock doors open. You can't see them from the street."

Carlotti scowled. "So?"

"That means you entered the parking area. That's the only way to see the loading dock. The only reason you'd come into the parking area would be if you were meeting someone."

"I already told you I was meeting Nathan."

Hench jumped in. "You met Nathan?" He turned to me. "She was here that night? She killed Nathan? Have you told the police yet?"

"Not quite. See, the question is, why was she meeting Sloan in your lab? Or, more important, why did Sloan arrange for her to meet him here instead of anywhere else?"

Hench looked around his lab then shrugged. "Why was Nathan meeting her anywhere? He shouldn't be talking to this woman in the first place. And he certainly shouldn't have let her into our research facility."

"That's true. Of course, he was already supplying Sophia's organization with inside information about Highland."

Carlotti's scowl deepened while Hench shook his head and said, "That's ridiculous."

"Oh, no. It's quite true. Sloan and a man by the name of Jeffrey Henderson were working together. Jeffrey was Sophia's right-hand man. Until he was murdered."

Hench flinched. "Murdered? What's that got to do with Sloan's being killed by Carlotti? Did this crazy woman kill both of them?"

I studied the mice, rats, and monkeys in their cages. Most were dozing, but a few were watching us as if we were their evening's entertainment. "I don't think so." I worked my way around the lab and now leaned against the door that led to the hallway. I hoped Hench would swivel and put his back to the loading dock. "You see, Sloan suspected something was wrong with the medical trial results coming out of Highland. He discussed this with a colleague. Remember Dr. Ingrid Olsson? Well, she happened to be Jeffrey Henderson's mother."

Hench's jaw dropped. "Ingrid...and Henderson..."

"Yep. Which brings us back to why Dr. Sloan and Carlotti were meeting at your lab that night. Especially given that you're the one who conducts the final animal trials and you're the one who gets the biggest bonus for every drug that advances to human trials."

Hench crossed his arms. "What are you insinuating?"

"Sloan thought you were cooking the books, so to speak. Faking test results. Maybe even swapping out sick animals with healthy ones. That would sure account for some of the increase in your orders for test animals." I tilted my head toward Carlotti. "The animals that Sophia rescued from your lab miraculously recovered once out of your care. I'm sure the FDA would be interested in that."

"That's ridiculous. Those animals were at the end of the drug trial. Of course they recovered. The drug worked. They were cured."

"That's what you told the techs who went to pick up the animals. But it wasn't true. They weren't the same animals you started with. You only started to test Dr. Sloan's newest drug therapy two months before. According to his notes, it took at least five months of treatment before the animals responded. Sloan knew you were pushing drugs out the door without proper testing. And he brought Sophia here to show her the evidence."

Hench scoffed. "That's stupid. Why wouldn't he come to me? Why wouldn't he go to the FDA? Why would he take that to some muckraker?"

"Dr. Olsson described Sloan as a dedicated researcher. He was looking for a cure for a disease that killed one of his children. If he went to you, what would stop you from firing him? Discrediting him? Any accusations he brought up after that would be coming from a disgruntled employee. Nobody would take him seriously."

Hench pressed his hands on the stainless-steel island and leaned toward me. "You're out of your mind. I'm going to make sure you're raked over the coals in the press for such baseless and criminal accusations. You'll never hold elected office again."

"You need to come up with a better threat than that." I stepped away from the door and positioned myself so that I was on the opposite side of the table from Hench. Carlotti moved to the same side of the island as Hench but closer to the animal cages. The three of us formed an equilateral triangle with the worktable in its center. "What made you come back to your lab that night? Was it that extra shipment of animals coming in? Were you planning on swapping out even more of your test animals? Sophia saw the loaded tractor-trailer. It pulled into the driveway before suddenly reversing and racing down the street. Did you call off the delivery after shooting Sloan?"

Hench's face twitched. "There's no proof of anything you said."

"There will be when Carlotti and I go to the police and bring Sloan's research assistant in with us. The police will check with the delivery company and see if they took animals away from the lab every time they delivered a special order for you. Next, they'll examine your lab records and your financials. All the proof is in there. That's what Ingrid Olsson found, isn't it? That's why you killed her, too."

"You're as much of a nut case as Carlotti. Get the hell out of my lab."

"I forgot one other piece of evidence. An eyewitness."

He laughed. "You mean that piece-of-trash janitor? She's the one who's toting a gun. When the police find her, she'll have a lot of explaining to do."

"That woman happens to be my sister-in-law. She'll identify you as the shooter."

"That's only if she's found alive, and I've got someone on that problem." Hench whipped his hand behind his back and pulled his gun out of its concealed holster. He swung the gun side to side so that it covered both Carlotti and me. "I'm sure the police will understand that I was nervous when I saw two intruders in my lab. Both of you came in through the loading dock. Your fingerprints will show that. I'll be within my rights to protect myself and my property."

He jerked his head to indicate that Carlotti should move closer to me. She merely slid her hands into her pockets and stayed where she was. He raised the gun higher.

A scraping sound from the loading dock made the three of us jerk our heads in that direction. Ben and Caleb stood in the open doorway.

"Damn it," Hench shouted and swung his gun toward the newcomers.

"No," I shouted as I vaulted over the island and launched myself toward Hench.

Two shots rang out simultaneously.

I felt a burning pain. I touched the wound, and my hand came away sticky with blood. I passed out.

Chapter Twenty-Nine

When I awoke, I felt Alicia's hand in mine before I saw her. My unfocused eyes saw three dimly glowing figures around me as if guardian angels were surrounding my body. I blinked and the figures sharpened, which seemed to cause all of them to speak at once. I realized I was in a hospital room, hooked up to intravenous drip lines and monitors. I hoped it wasn't my heart this time.

"Shh," Alicia demanded of the others and stroked my forehead. "Looks like you're back in the land of the living. If you ever do anything so stupid again, you won't be here long because I'll personally kill you." She brought my hand to her lips and kissed it.

"Ben?"

"Here, Ma." One of the ghostly figures moved forward. I spotted Sarah beside him.

"It's all my fault," he said. "I'm so sorry. Caleb tried to tell me we should wait until the police got there, but I was worried. I couldn't just sit in the car."

"It's okay. The important thing is you weren't hurt. What happened to everybody else?"

Ben and Alicia shared a silent moment of communication before Ben said, "Sophia shot Hench. He might not make it."

"Wouldn't be the first person I've killed." Carlotti strolled into the hospital room. "Hopefully, it will be the last. Damn hard shot to make, too. Tough to hit him without nicking you, but I guess old training kicks in when you really need it." She looked me up and down. "Wanted to make sure you came through all right. That was one hell of a leap you made. Right into the bullet. A little to the right or left, and it'd be your kid in that bed instead of you. Actually, he'd probably be in the morgue."

Alicia groaned and tightened her grasp on my hand.

Carlotti wasn't finished with her report. "That son of a

bitch Hench killed Jeff, too. The police found a ghost gun at Hench's home. Usually those do-it-yourself guns don't leave rifling marks on bullets, but whoever put this one together left a distinctive groove in the barrel. The police matched it to the bullet they found in Jeff."

"I thought so," I said. "When I was told Jeffrey met with Hench, I figured he'd shown Hench at least part of his evidence. Hench must have set up the meeting for a deserted area of Oak Park, figuring he might have to shoot Jeffrey if he really had any evidence. Probably took whatever it was with him after killing Jeffrey."

"Makes sense," Carlotti said. "Don't know why he sent Peter Nevin to rip through my office, though."

"And through Jeffrey's apartment." I threw out the scenario I'd concocted in my musings with Ginger. "Jeffrey talked to John Johnson, a reporter, and told him about having evidence against Highland. Johnson mentioned it to me, so I'm sure he mentioned it to Hench when he interviewed him after Sloan's murder. It would have gotten Hench to thinking about possible additional evidence and where it might be."

"Which led him to my office where somebody did find the papers Jeff asked me to hide." Carlotti eyed me. "Since they didn't go missing, it probably wasn't Hench."

I tried to keep my face impassive, which was easier to do with painkillers running through my veins.

Alicia broke in. "At least Nevin is off the streets. He'll lose his license over this one for sure."

"I think jail time for breaking and entering might also figure into his future," I said.

Carlotti said, "I thought you'd want to know that the police have called in the FDA, the PHS, the OLAW, and the FBI. All those initials will be digging into Hench's schemes. Turns out, faking drug results wasn't his only avenue for extra income. That slime ball owned the Santa Barbara ranch where all the smuggled exotic animals were rescued, and there's a strong suspicion that most of them came from his spread in Brazil. The FBI is working with police in Brazil to investigate Hench's ranch there. All in all, a good day's work. And since Highland is now officially out of business, I need to make sure the lab animals that can be saved are taken care of." She turned to leave.

When she reached the door, she turned back to say, "By the way, Johnny Johnson says hello, and he'd like to interview you for the exposé he's writing on Highland. He might even have enough material to write a book."

"Was he working with you this whole time?"

"No. He had his own axe to grind about Highland. He and Jeff talked, but they were on two different tracks. Who knew those trains led to the same depot?" Carlotti left without a wave.

I turned to Alicia. "What about Michelle?"

"She's safe. She and Lefty got the message from the tattooed guy at the warehouse. They finally used common sense and called Keesha. They'd been hiding in the house Keesha was watching, so she picked them up and took them to our place."

A hundred other questions whirled through my mind, but the drugs swept over me and I slid into sleep with my family beside me.

****

The oak paneling in Judge Quentin Jefferson's office gave a warm glow to the light and airy sanctuary. Bookcases filled with leather-bound legal tomes filled the walls behind Quentin's desk. Bird songs filtered in from the open windows of the side wall. Sunbeams from those windows highlighted Alicia's profile and made Ben's eyes sparkle. I wanted to wrap both of them in my arms and never let go. Instead, I concentrated on imprinting each and every sight and sound of this in the permanent storage area of my brain.

Alicia and I flanked Ben as we sat in wooden chairs facing Quentin, who sat behind his sturdy desk. In back of us, I heard Amy as she squirmed in her mother's arms. David cooed soothing noises to her.

Quentin beamed at us all. "This is quite the occasion, and I'm honored and delighted that the family courts allowed me to officiate at this adoption proceeding. Not my usual criminal caseload, I'm glad to say, but they briefed me on all their customary procedures." He picked up a stack of papers and tapped them on his desk until they formed a neat pile. "For the record, all the legal documents are duly filed and recorded. Now I have to ask you, Katherine Matthews, are you adopting Benjamin Wise of your own free will?"

"I am. Proudly."

"And you, Alicia Wise, approve of your spouse adopting Ben?"

Alicia returned Quentin's smile. "I do."

"Finally, Benjamin, is it your wish to be adopted by Katherine Matthews who will share joint custodial rights with your mother, Alicia?"

Ben faced me and said, "It is."

"Then I congratulate this newly legal family that has, in reality, existed for many decades. And, as is the tradition of the family court system here in Santa Barbara County, I want to give the adoptee a special gift." Quentin reached behind him and brought out a wicker basket filled with stuffed toys. "You get your pick, Ben."

As Ben pulled out a purple dragon, everyone erupted into applause.

We gathered in front of Quentin's desk for a photo. Ben stood between me and Alicia. I tried to hide my arm sling behind Ben, but he pushed me forward and wrapped an arm around Alicia and me.

Ben kissed my forehead. "You should be proud of what you did to save your family."

Michelle, with a fresh haircut and a new outfit, stood beside Alicia. Quentin flanked her. Sarah, holding Amy, stood on my left with David beside her. Before a neatly-groomed Lefty even tried to take the picture, everyone was demanding his or her own copy.

"C'mon," Ben said. "Caleb's holding down the fort at the restaurant. I don't trust him not to eat all the food before we get there."

Caleb had, indeed, been preparing the celebration at the restaurant. Balloons and flowers filled the small private room, and a buffet service was set out along one wall. A wonderful aroma met us at the door to the room.

Caleb came up to me and said, "Thanks for inviting me to this. It feels special to be at such a family event."

"It was Ben's idea, but you've certainly earned a place at the table. Thanks for taking care of me and Ben. I know you're the one who kept me from bleeding out while the ambulance was on its way. To say I owe you is an understatement."

"It was really Ben who kept the pressure on. I hear you've got a long recovery ahead, but that you'll be good as new in a few months."

"More like six. Us old folks don't heal as quickly." I looked around and dropped my voice. "Have you heard anything about the mess at Highland?"

"Yeah. Hench was scamming the system for money. He substituted perfectly healthy animals for the ones his lab techs infected with the disease. Then he gave the new animals low doses of whatever drug he was supposed to be testing so it would show up if the animals were autopsied. He also had drugs on hand to counteract the chemo drugs in case the animals got too sick. That was the list you found. Jeff must have discovered the list but not known what it meant."

"Much like yours truly. I can't believe it took me so long to put everything together. I mean, the first time I talked to Hench he told me it usually took three-and-a-half years to get a drug to human trials. But Highland was only open a year and a half. That wasn't enough time to develop two drugs, let alone have two more on the way. It didn't compute."

"Hench wasn't the only one cheating. Two of the other researchers brought possible drugs with them when they joined Highland. They stole them from their previous jobs. That's why the initial testing went so fast. Even though my research with Sloan wasn't part of that, I should have seen it." Caleb shook his head mournfully.

"I suppose they consoled themselves with the reward they received for creating a new drug."

"Yeah. I heard that Sloan paid off his ex-wife with one of his bonuses. Maybe that's why he was conflicted about calling in the FDA." Caleb grimaced. "The things people will do, or ignore, for money."

"Do you happen to know if the dead body the hikers found was ever identified? Was it Dr. Olsson?"

Caleb's eyes widened. "How did you know? I just saw

the news a few minutes ago while I was waiting for you guys to get here." He dug his phone out of his pocket and scrolled through several pages before handing it to me.

The news bulletin from the police department stated the dead woman was identified as Dr. Ingrid Olsson through DNA testing. Her face was disfigured and acid applied to her fingers to erase her fingerprints. No suspects for the crime were mentioned.

I handed Caleb his phone. "I'm sorry my hunch was right."

"How did you figure it out?"

"Timing, mainly. Olsson disappeared soon after I heard her suggest to Hench that something was wrong with the orders. She didn't resign in person. The only communication was an email from her phone that anyone could have sent."

"Anyone, meaning her killer?"

"Makes sense to me. Also, she worked with Sloan, and he probably told her his suspicions about Hench faking the final test results. I'm guessing that confronting Hench about that wouldn't be a safe thing to do."

"If Hench recovers, I'm sure that's one of the many questions the police will have for him."

I thought of the total waste of human and animal life caused by his greed and shook my head.

Caleb broke into my morose thoughts. "Did Ben tell you about my new job? I'm going to be a research assistant at UCSB while I work on my doctorate. I applied a month ago. Finally got the word this morning."

"Congratulations. The university has a reputation for doing amazing research." I hesitated. "Are animals involved?"

"Probably. But I'm working with Animals First to find alternatives as much as possible."

I thought Ben would appreciate that.

Michelle picked that moment to hand me a glass of apple cider in a flute. Caleb patted my good shoulder and left as Michelle said, "No champagne for you with those pain pills. Or for me with my cacophony of meds."

It was marvelous to see her with clear eyes and some color in her cheeks. "You're looking good. How did the police interview go this morning?"

"Follow-up questions. They wanted to make sure I could identify Hench as the one who went into the lab. They asked again about the argument I heard and about how and why I hid in the utility closet after I heard the shot and why I took off the company shirt before I ran." She snorted. "Like I'd stand in the hallway waiting for the jerk with a gun to come out and find me there? Like I wanted to be easily identified as a Premier Cleaning Services worker once I got out the door? Sheesh." She took a sip. "This time they didn't press me about having a gun. I think that lawyer of yours kind of scared them off that line of inquiry."

"That's the third time they've run you through all that."

"I think they want it all on record in case there's a trial," Michelle said. "They seem to have some fear that I might suddenly disappear. I can't imagine why."

We gave each other wry grins.

I spotted Lefty in the food line. He sported new slacks and shirt as well as a fresh haircut. He cleaned up well. "Did Lefty ever tell you why he left San Diego?"

"He had an episode. They happen, but less often now." Michelle took another sip of cider. "He was heading back to our apartment from work, and he saw three women in hijabs holding packages. He flashed to his last patrol in   Afghanistan. Half his men were killed when some women on the street exploded IEDs they'd hidden under their robes. He figured these women carried bombs, too, so he ran and kept running. Ended up on a bus to Santa Barbara. He was still pretty out of it when I found him at the warehouse. Shocked to see me. He somehow thought I'd been killed in his   imaginary blast."

I thought of Zach, who entered the in-patient treatment center for counseling. I wondered if it would help Lefty. "I'm glad the two of you are staying with us."

"So am I. For the moment." Michelle gestured toward the food. "Since you're impaired, let me bring you a plate of food."

"Thanks."

Ben tapped a fork against his water glass. We all quieted down and turned to him.

"First of all, thank you for helping me celebrate my   adoption." Cheers interrupted until Ben held up his hand. "I want to tell you this is the family I've been blessed with all my life. But it's wonderful to have the legal documents to make it official.

"I've decided to legally change my name as well. I'm going to take the name of my grandfather, Kate's dad, as my middle name. My last name will be the hyphenated maiden names of my moms. So, let me present to you, Benjamin Christopher Mazer-Matthews." He bowed as we all clapped.

I felt an arm brush against mine. I looked to my left to see Sarah snuggling Amy to her chest. I chucked my   grandchild under her chin and was rewarded with a wide, toothless grin.

Sarah sighed. "I still don't know I agree with this, but I can see Ben is really happy."

I nodded. "Sometimes people we love make choices we don't agree with. Our job is to love them anyway."

Sarah gave me a wicked smile. "I'm glad you feel that way because Animals First has a protest march planned for next Saturday at Shoreline Park. David's coming and Ben and Caleb, too. And Amy's finally going to be able to wear her adorable ground squirrel costume. Wanna join us?"

My only response was a groan.

"How can a wild woman who deliberately leapt into the path of a bullet be such a wuss about attending a protest?" Sarah's look was one of mock despair that morphed into a mischievous grin." Sarah's look was one of mock despair. "By the way, Sophia Carlotti is a new client of mine. We're going to get animal testing completely banned—first in California and then in the whole country."

"You know you'll be opposed by every pharmaceutical company in the world along with most universities and medical centers, right?

A defiant glint flashed in Sarah's eyes. "So? You always told us it was better to do what's right than to do what's easy."

Damn, I thought. Since when had she started listening to my homilies, let alone living by them?

I stifled my overprotective impulses and draped my good arm over Sarah's shoulders. "Unfortunately, it appears Joan of Arc's and Don Quixote's bloodlines run strong in this family. Who am I to argue with genetics?"

About the Author

Jane DiLucchio, a retired community college professor with a previous incarnation as an elementary school teacher, enjoys reading, cards games, theater-going, amateur farming, travel, food, wine, friends, and laughter. Jane, her wife, and their furry child make their home in southern California.

Bringing LGBTQAI+ Stories to Life

Visit us at our website: www.flashpointpublications.com

www.ingramcontent.com/pod-product-compliance
Lightning Source LLC
Chambersburg PA
CBHW070649100726
47907CB00007B/2147